JIMMY SNIFFLES A NOSE FOR DANGER

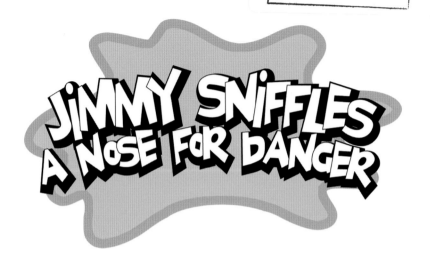

Librarian Reviewer

Laurie K. Holland

Media Specialist (National Board Certified), Edina, MN

MA in Elementary Education, Minnesota State University, Mankato, MN

Reading Consultant

Elizabeth Stedem

Educator/Consultant, Colorado Springs, CO

MA in Elementary Education, University of Denver, CO

Graphic Sparks are published by Stone Arch Books,
A Capstone Imprint
1710 Roe Crest Drive
North Mankato, Minnesota 56003.
www.capstonepub.com

Library of Congress Cataloging-in-Publication Data
Temple, Bob.
   A Nose for Danger / by Bob Temple; illustrated by Steve Harpster.
   p. cm. — (Graphic Sparks. Jimmy Sniffles)
   ISBN-13: 978-1-59889-036-5 (library binding)
   ISBN-10: 1-59889-036-0 (library binding)
   ISBN-13: 978-1-59889-171-3 (paperback)
   ISBN-10: 1-59889-171-5 (paperback)
   1. Graphic novels. I. Harpster, Steve. II. Title. III. Series.
PN6727.T2945J56 2006
741.5—dc22   2005026686

Summary: Jimmy Sniffles is allergic — to danger! ACHOOOO! A bag of diamonds is
missing from the local jewelry store, and Jimmy, with his super-snotty schnozz, saves the day.

Art Director: Heather Kindseth
Production Manager: Sharon Reid
Production/Design: James Liebman, Mie Tsuchida
Production Assistance: Bob Horvath, Eric Murray

Printed in the United States of America in North Mankato, Minnesota.
032016
009699R

JiMMY SNiFFLES
A Nose For Danger

BY BOB TEMPLE

ILLUSTRATED BY STEVE HARPSTER

STONE ARCH BOOKS
Minneapolis   San Diego

CAST OF CHARACTERS

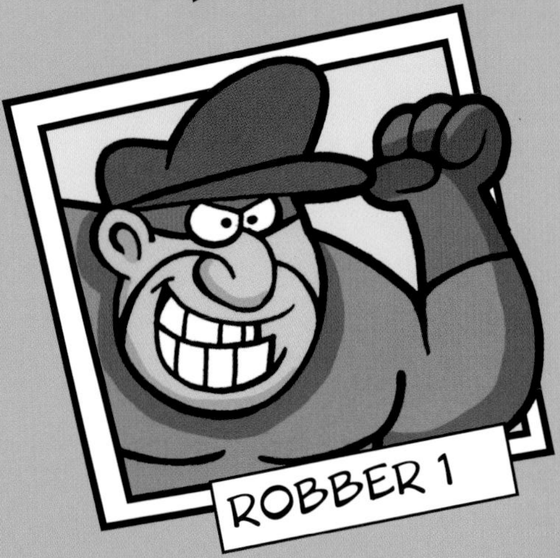
ROBBER 1

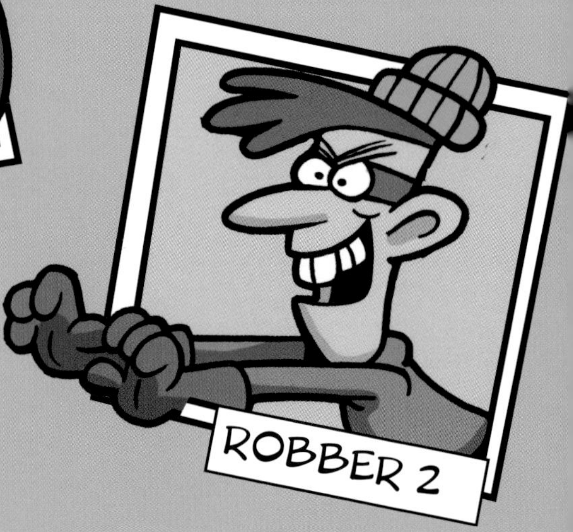
ROBBER 2

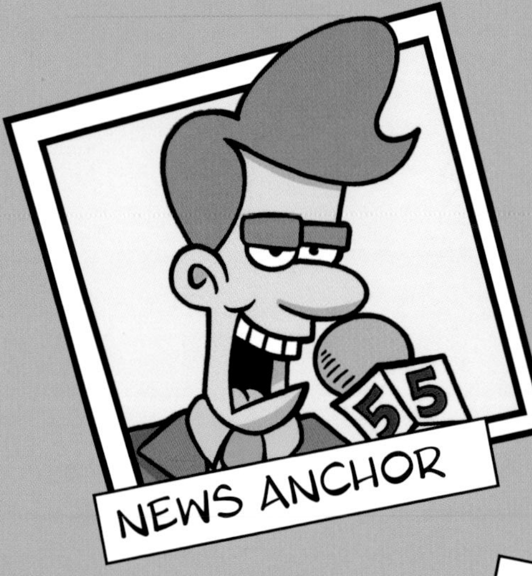
55
NEWS ANCHOR

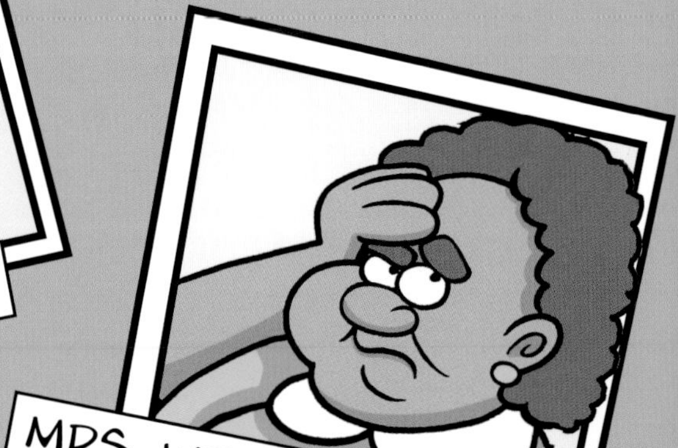
MRS. WINKLE

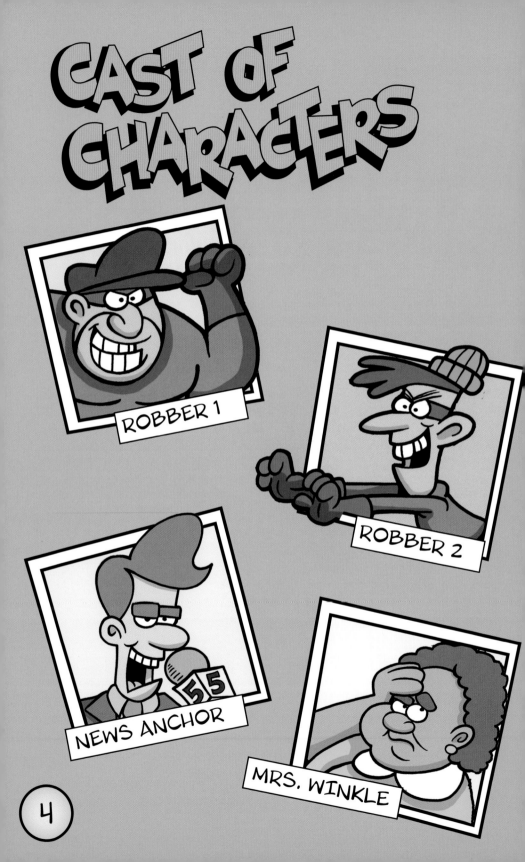

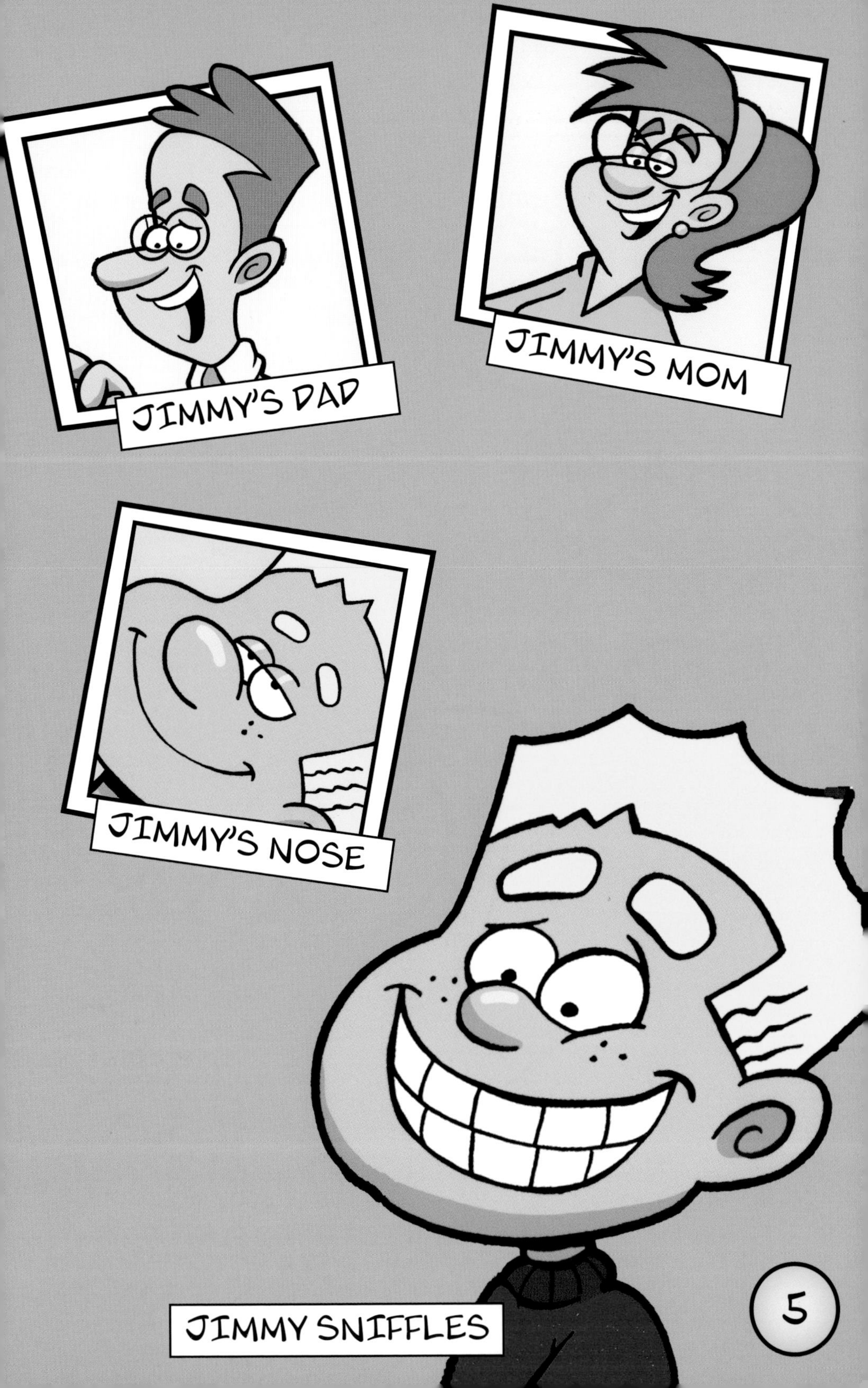
JIMMY'S DAD
JIMMY'S MOM
JIMMY'S NOSE
JIMMY SNIFFLES

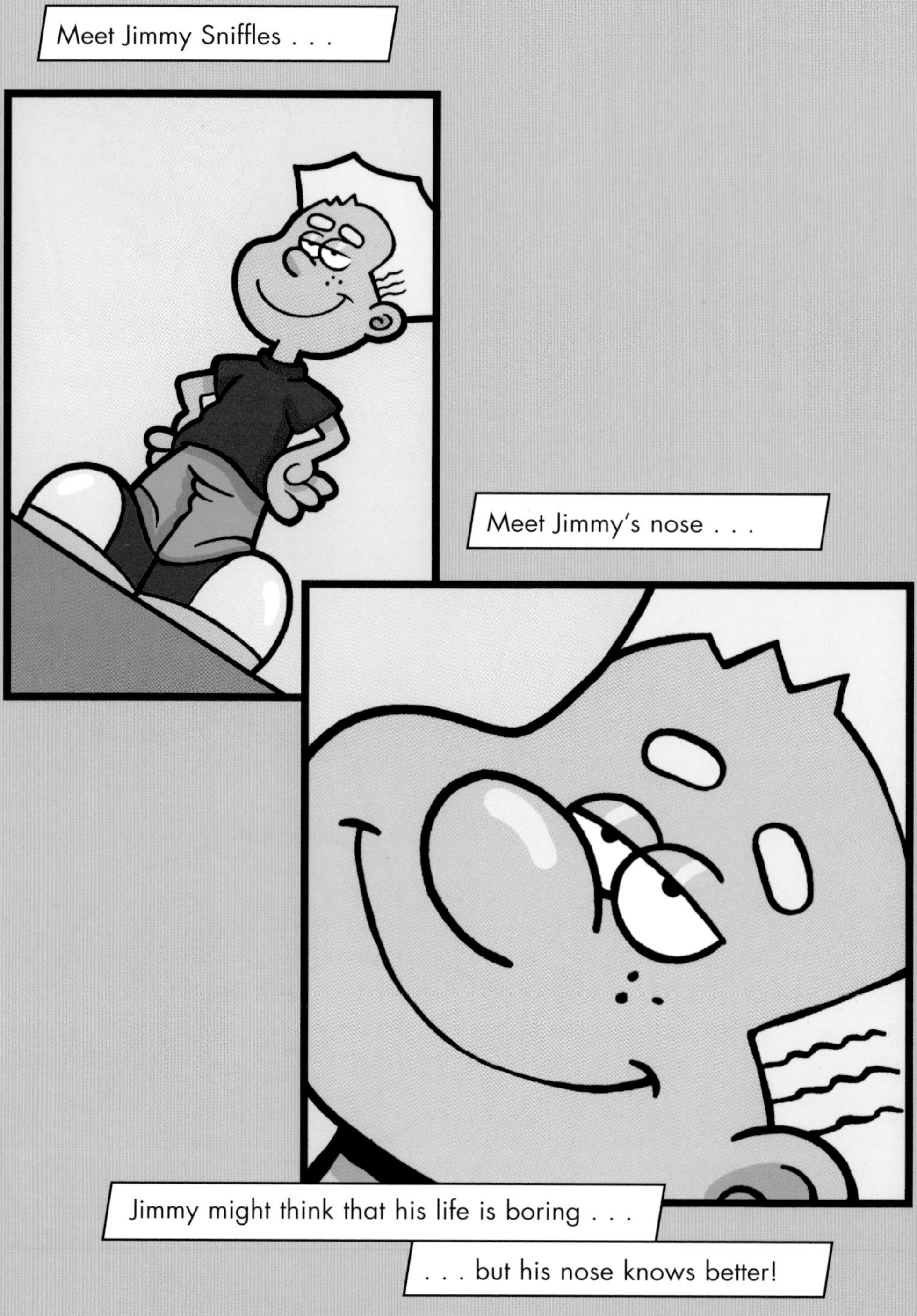
Meet Jimmy Sniffles . . .
Meet Jimmy's nose . . .
Jimmy might think that his life is boring . . .
. . . but his nose knows better!

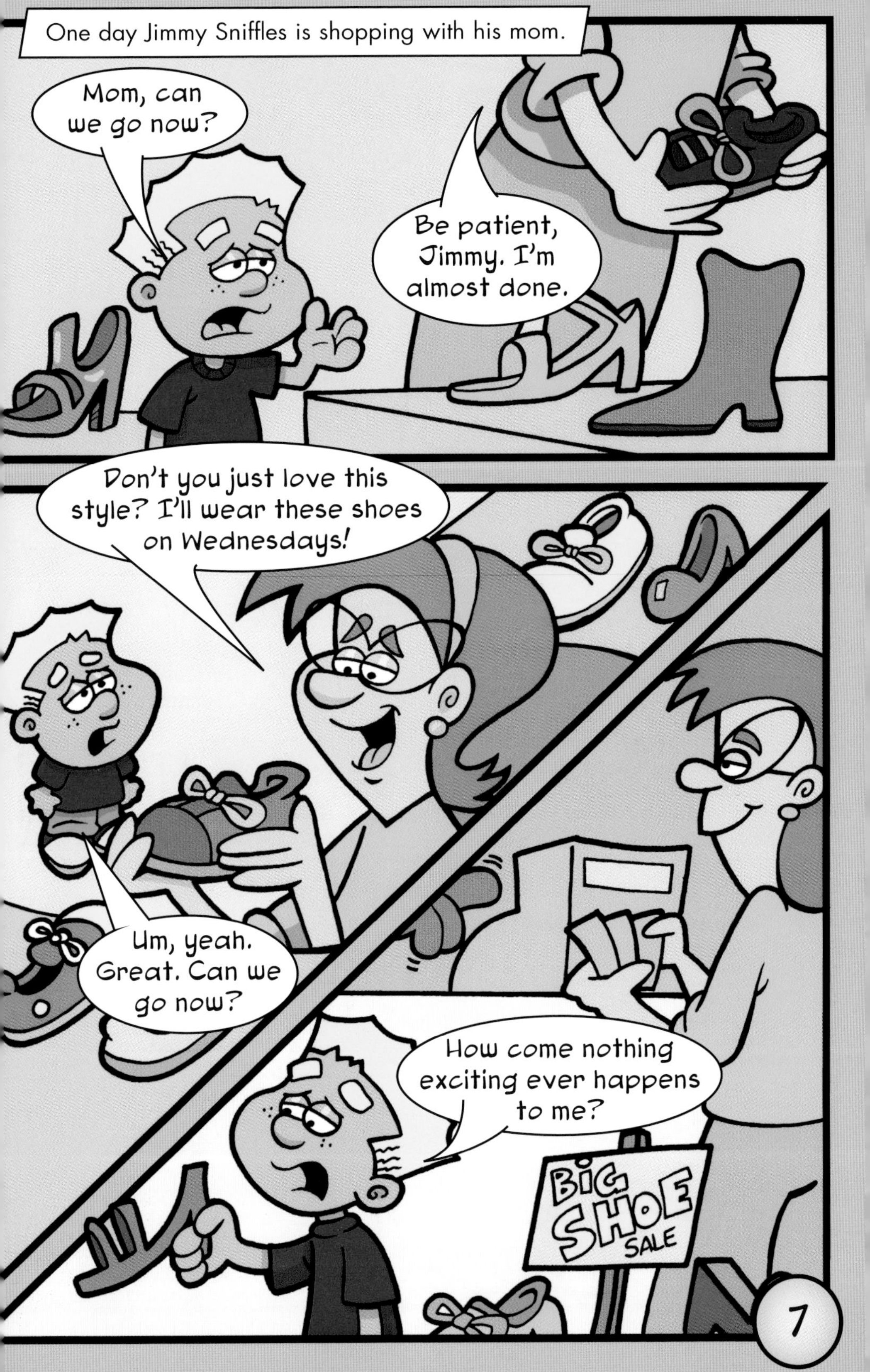

One day Jimmy Sniffles is shopping with his mom.
Mom, can we go now?
Be patient, Jimmy. I'm almost done.
Don't you just love this style? I'll wear these shoes on Wednesdays!
Um, yeah. Great. Can we go now?
How come nothing exciting ever happens to me?
BIG SHOE SALE

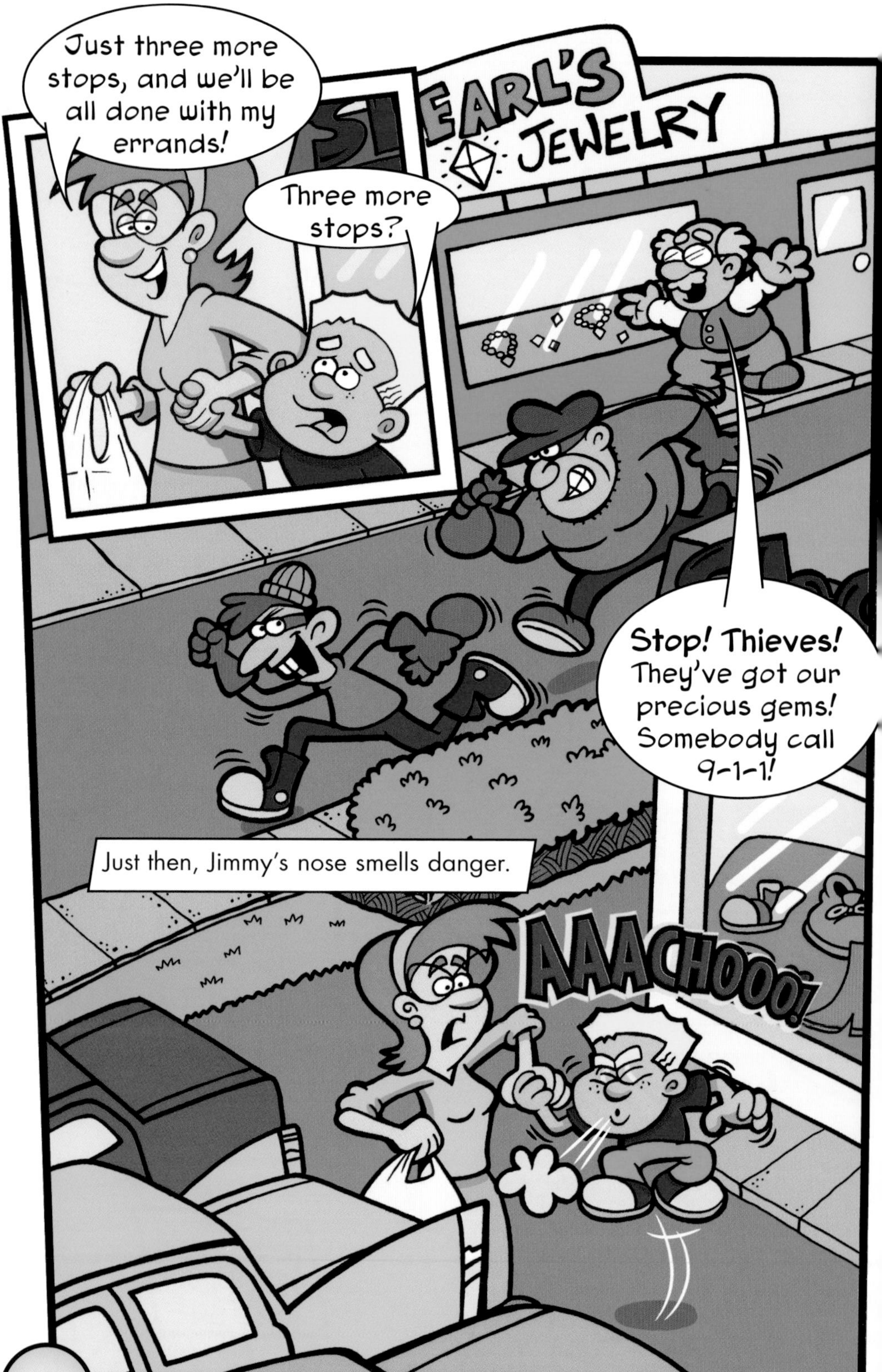
EARL'S JEWELRY
Just three more stops, and we'll be all done with my errands!
Three more stops?
Stop! Thieves! They've got our precious gems! Somebody call 9-1-1!
Just then, Jimmy's nose smells danger.
AAACHOOO!

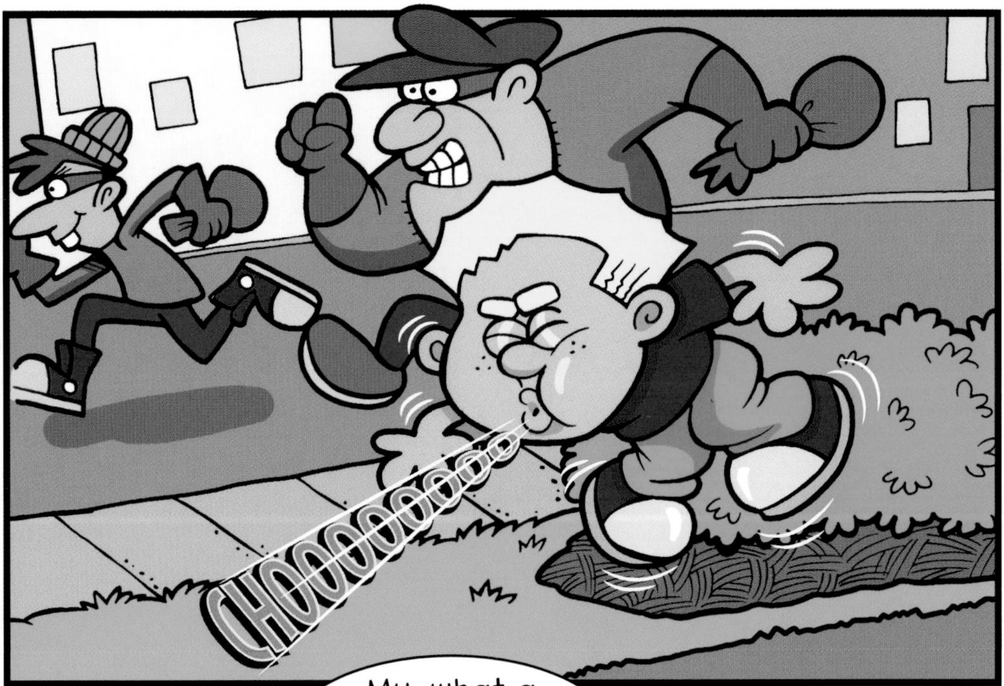
CHOOOOOOOO

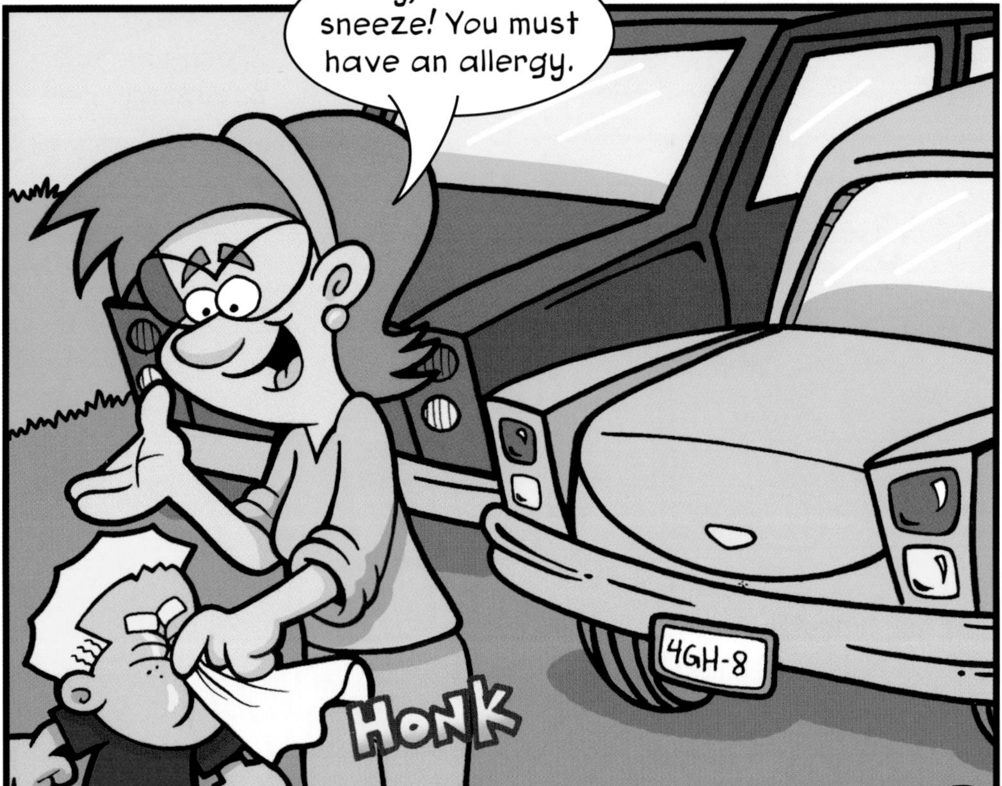
My, what a sneeze! You must have an allergy.
4GH-8
HONK

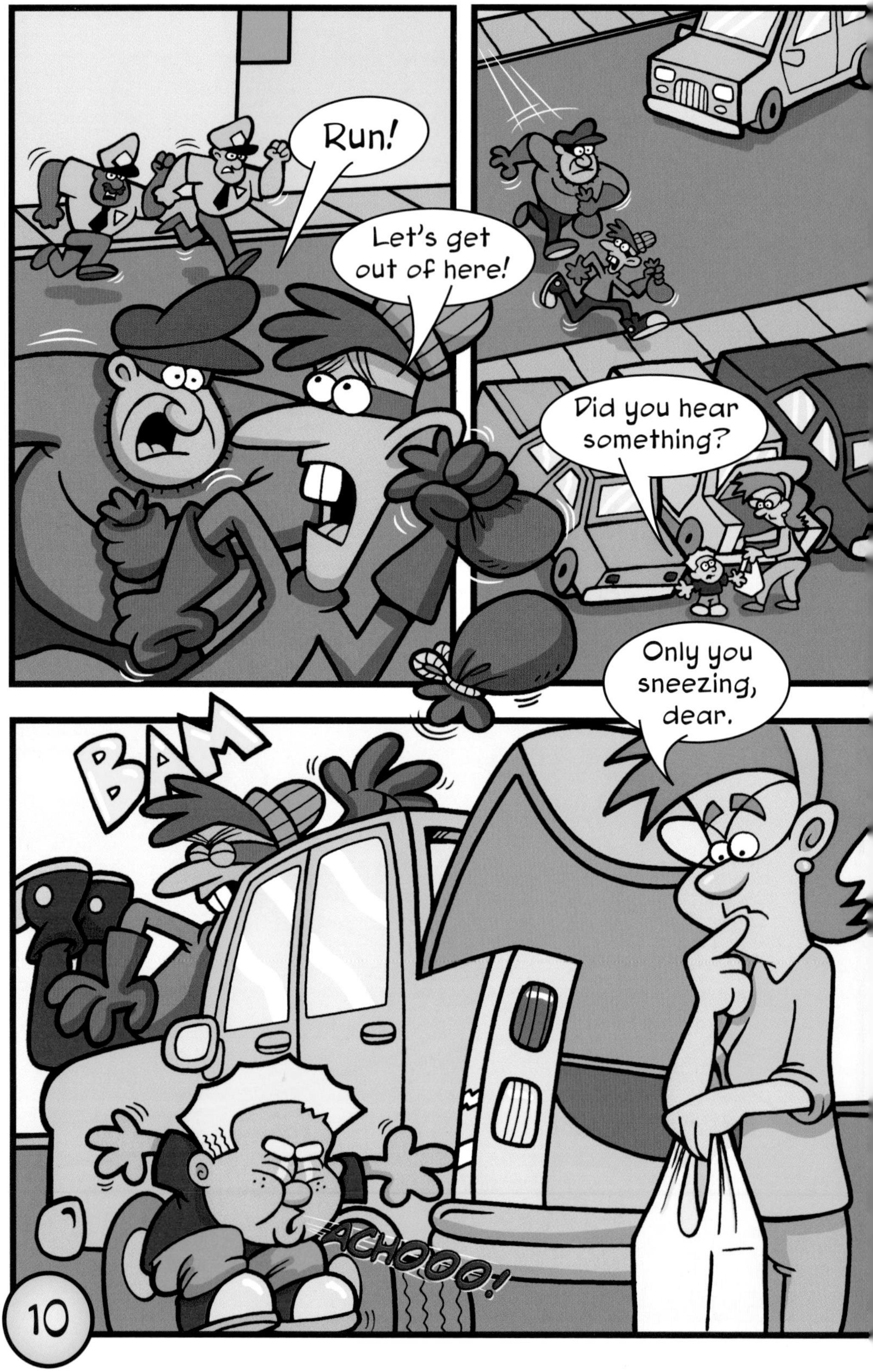
Run!
Let's get out of here!
Did you hear something?
Only you sneezing, dear.
BAM
ACHOOOO!

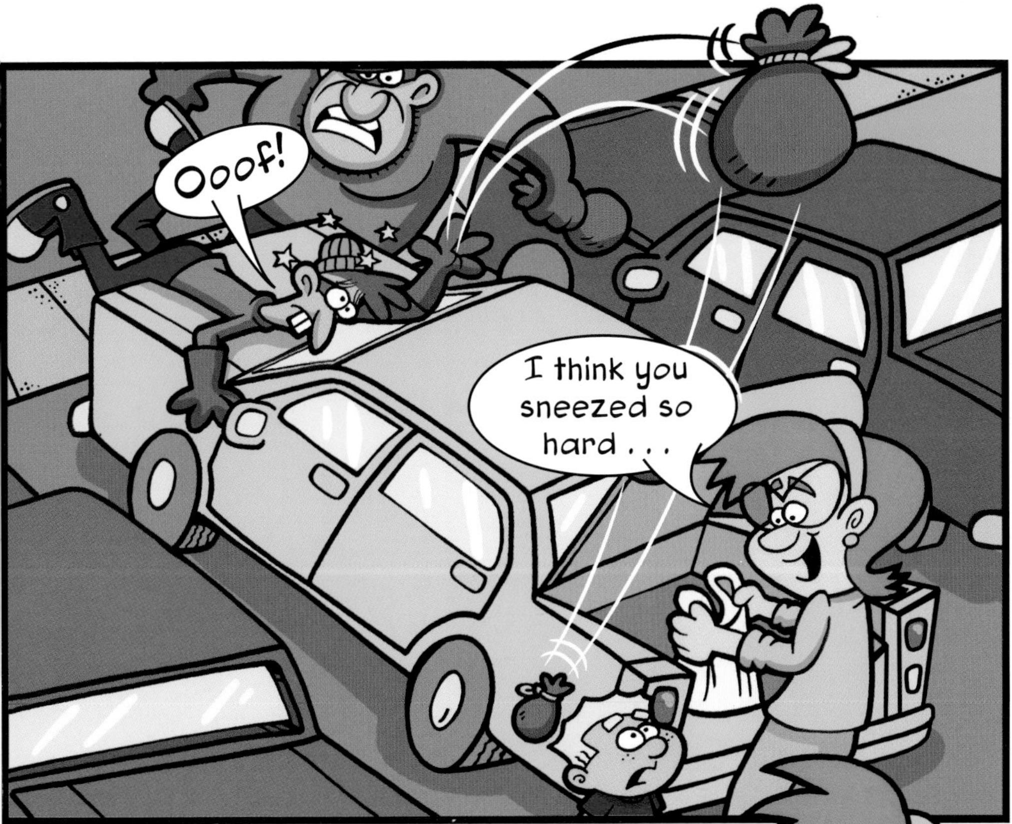
Ooof!
I think you sneezed so hard . . .

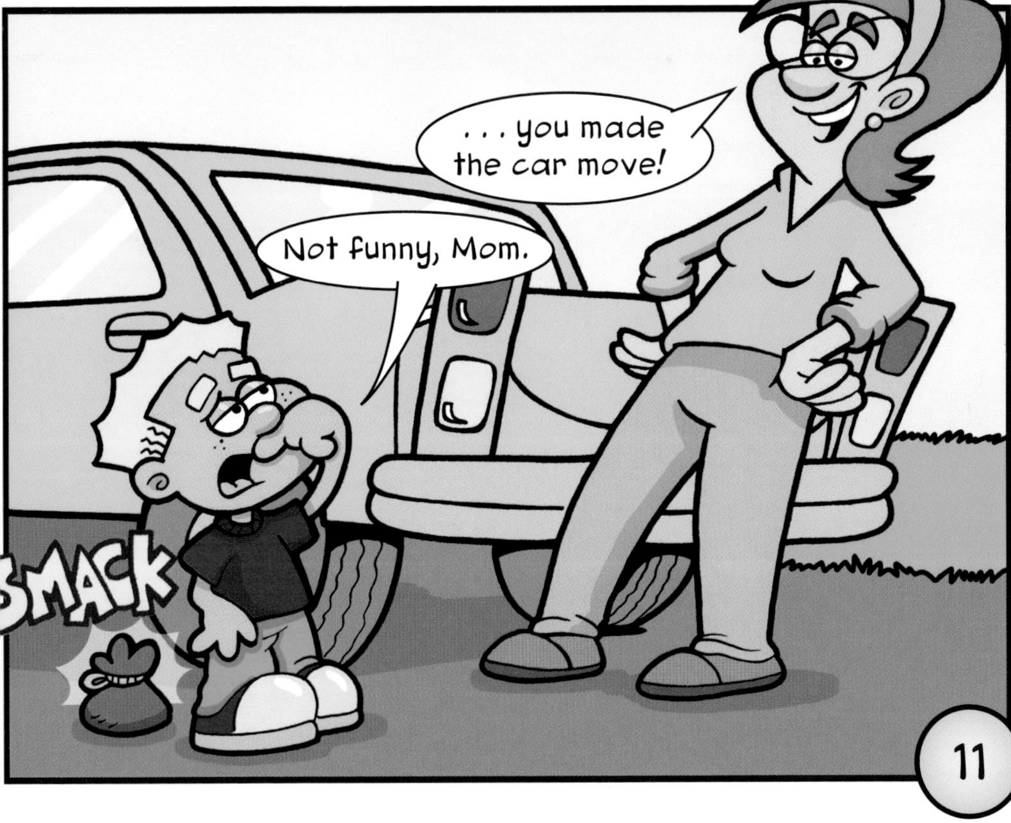
. . . you made the car move!
Not funny, Mom.
SMACK

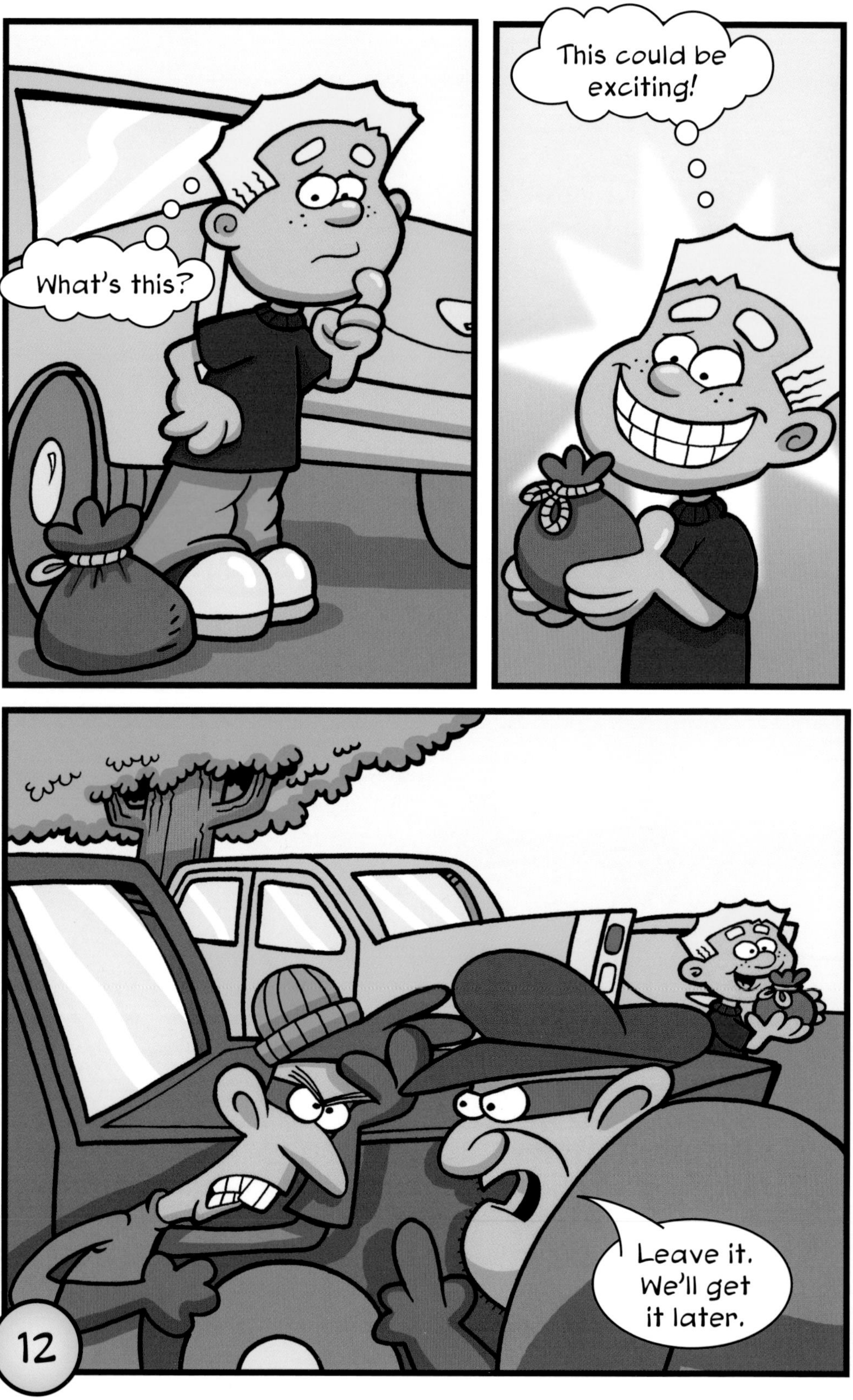
What's this?
This could be exciting!
Leave it. We'll get it later.

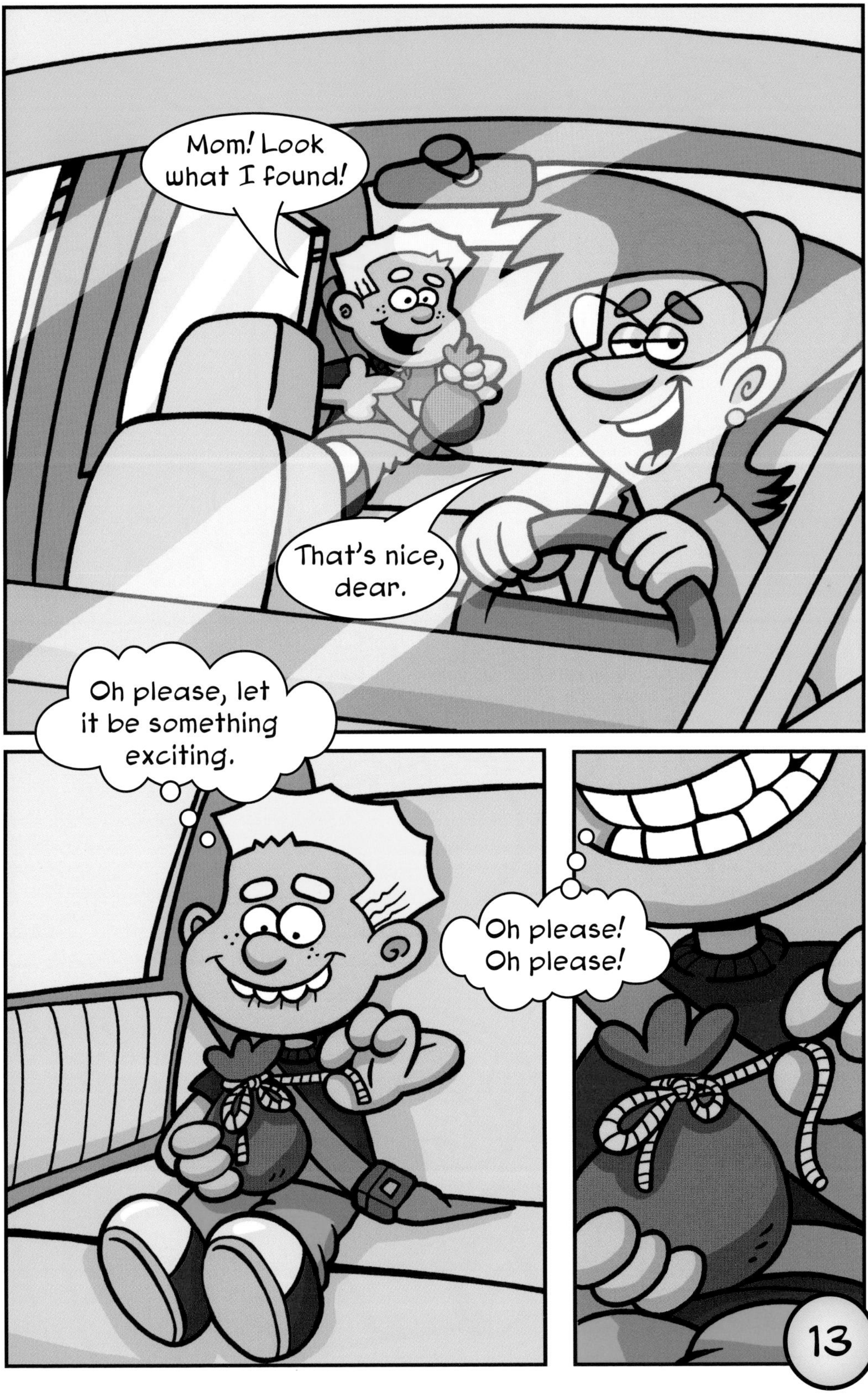
Mom! Look what I found!
That's nice, dear.
Oh please, let it be something exciting.
Oh please! Oh please!

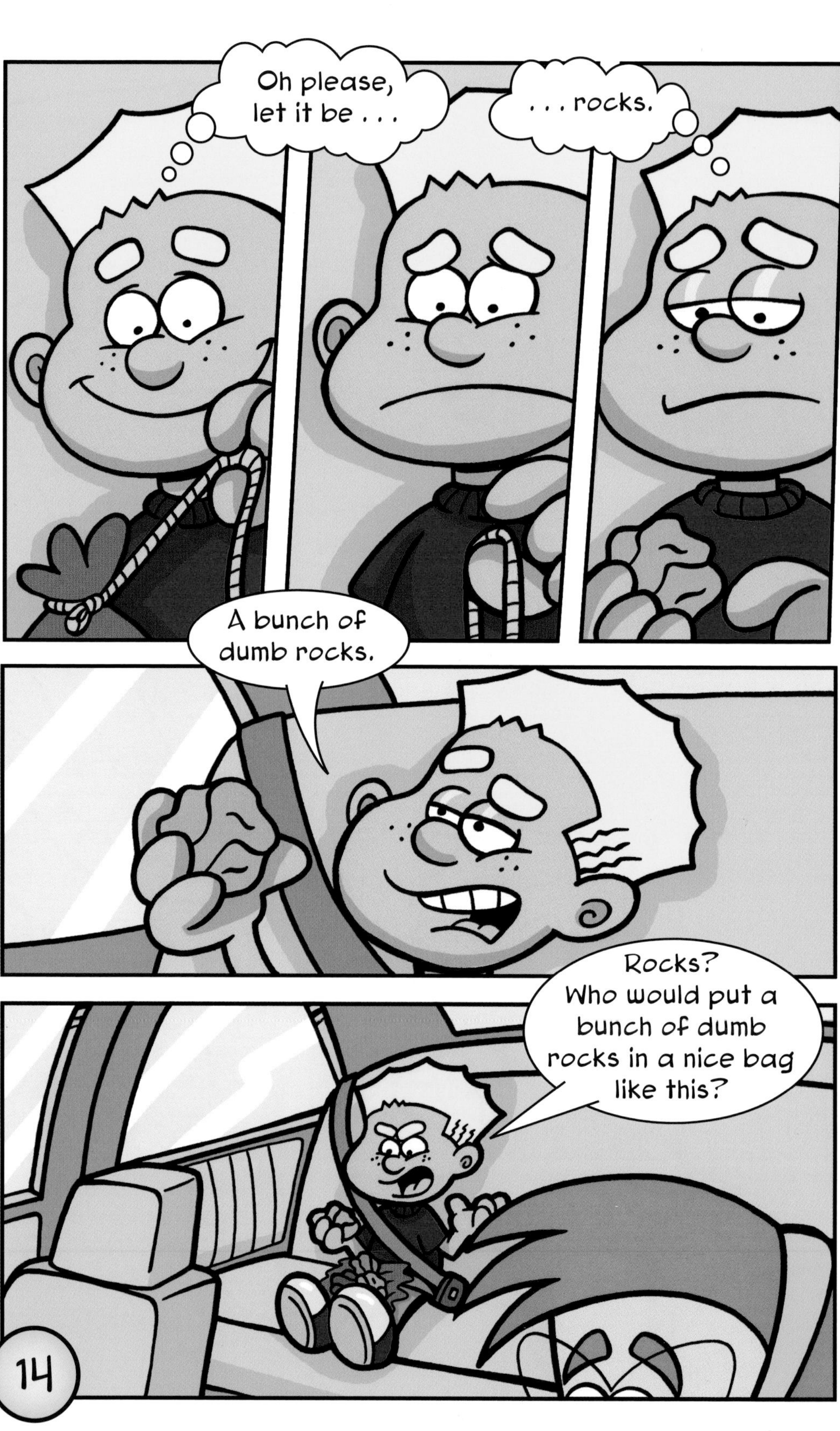
Oh please, let it be . . .
. . . rocks.
A bunch of dumb rocks.
Rocks? Who would put a bunch of dumb rocks in a nice bag like this?

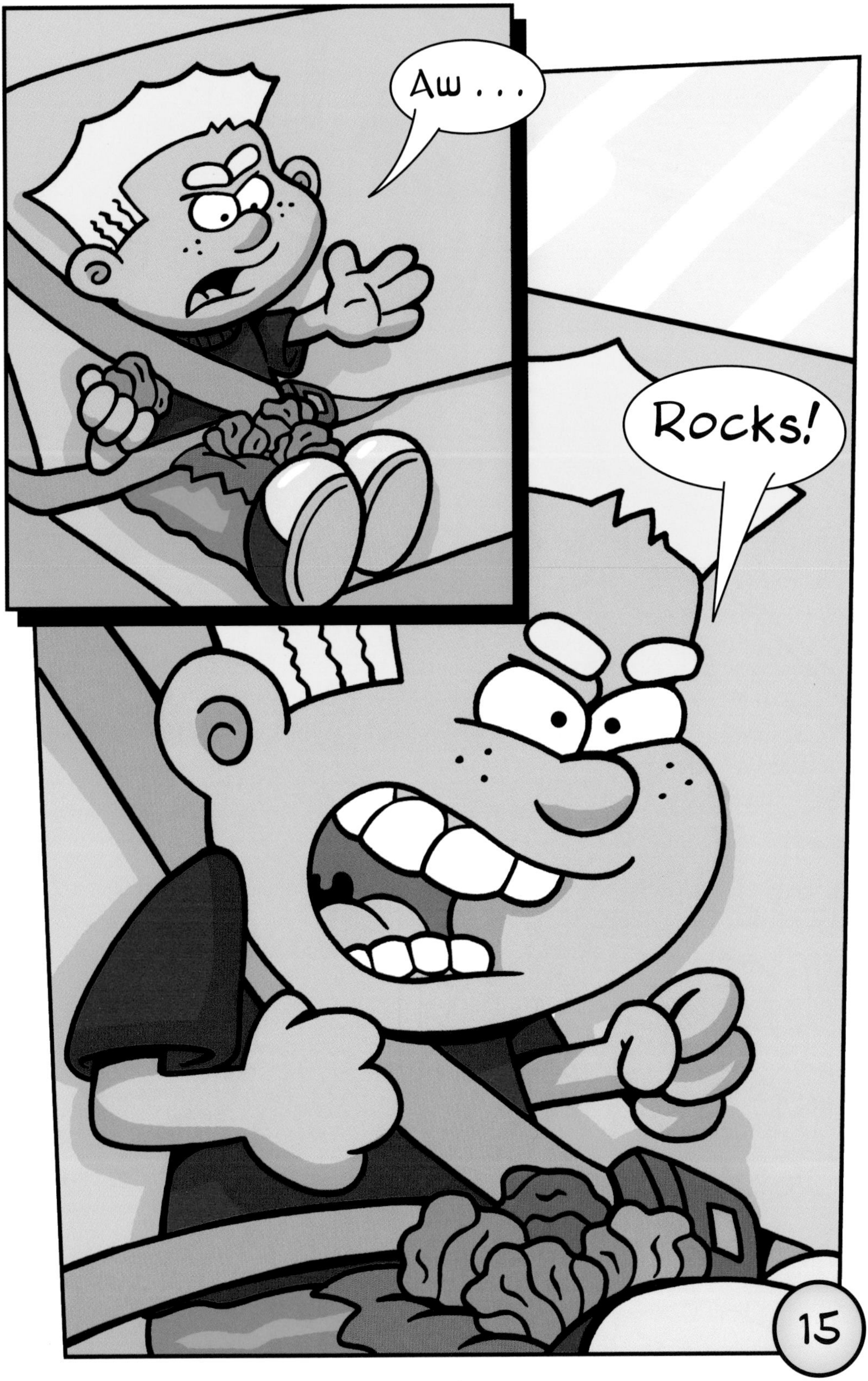
Aw . . .
Rocks!

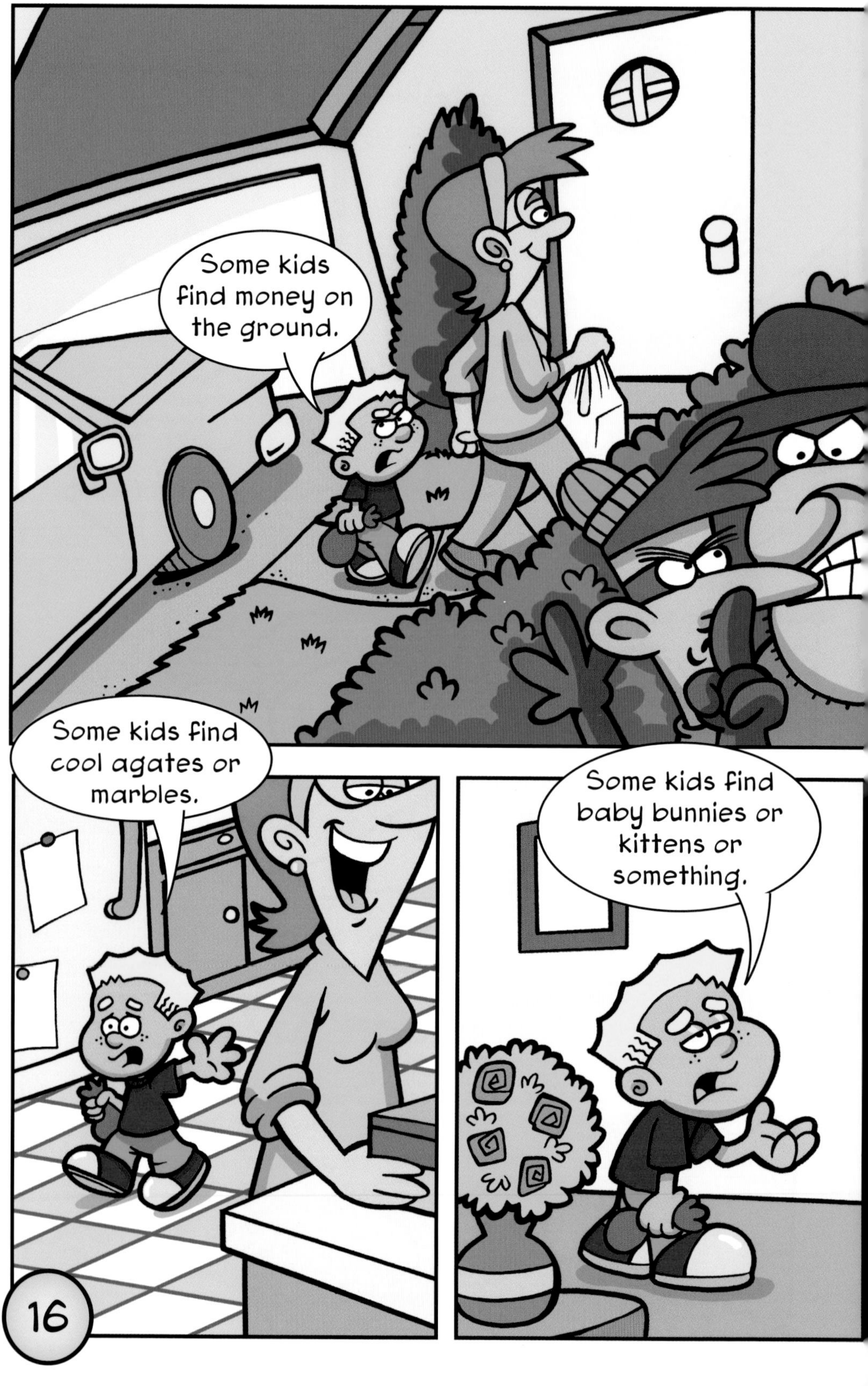
Some kids find money on the ground.
Some kids find cool agates or marbles.
Some kids find baby bunnies or kittens or something.

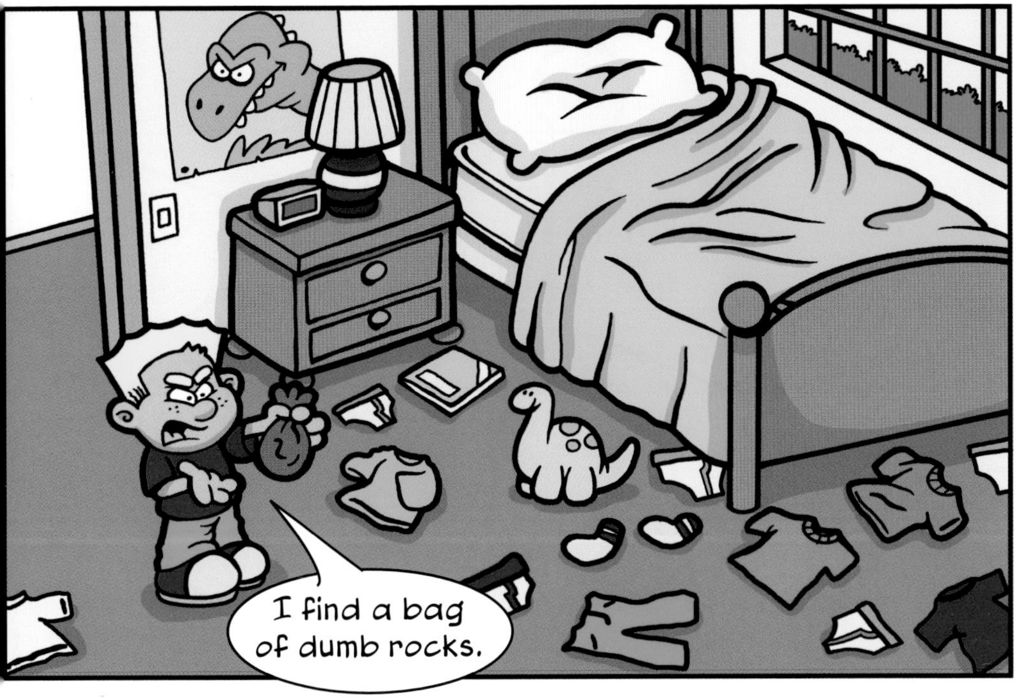
I find a bag
of dumb rocks.

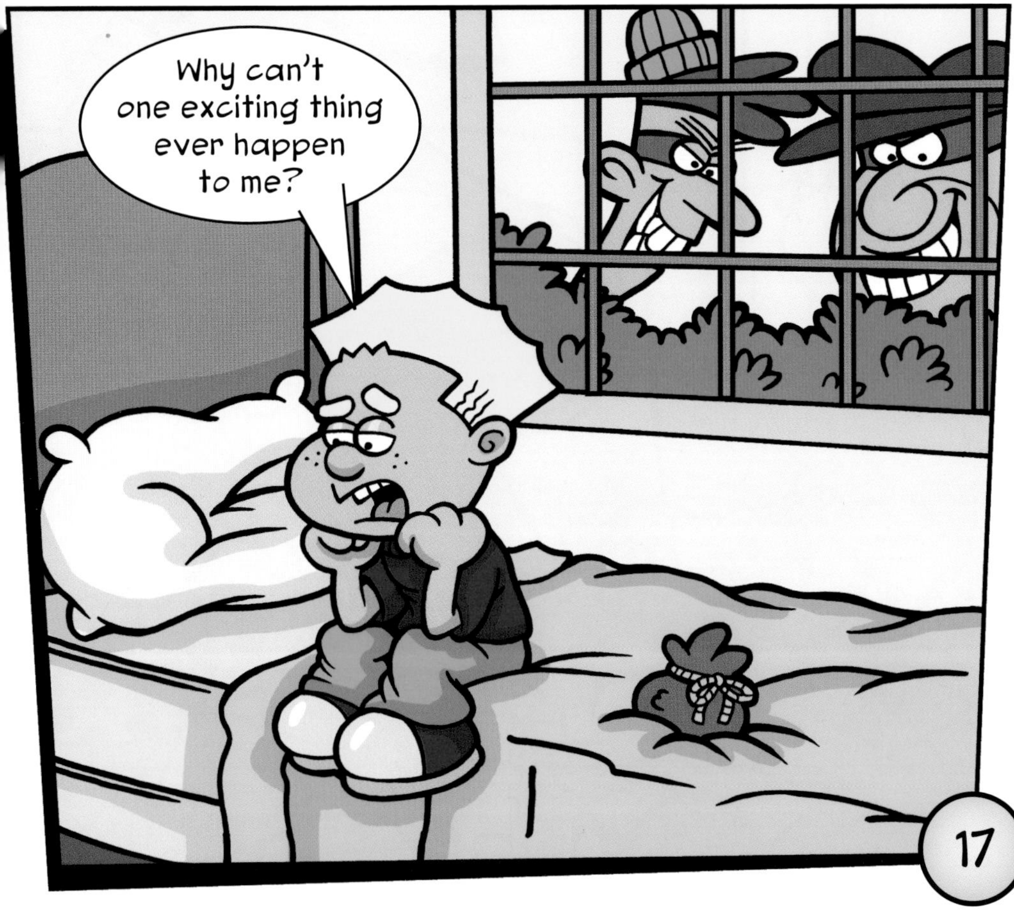
Why can't
one exciting thing
ever happen
to me?

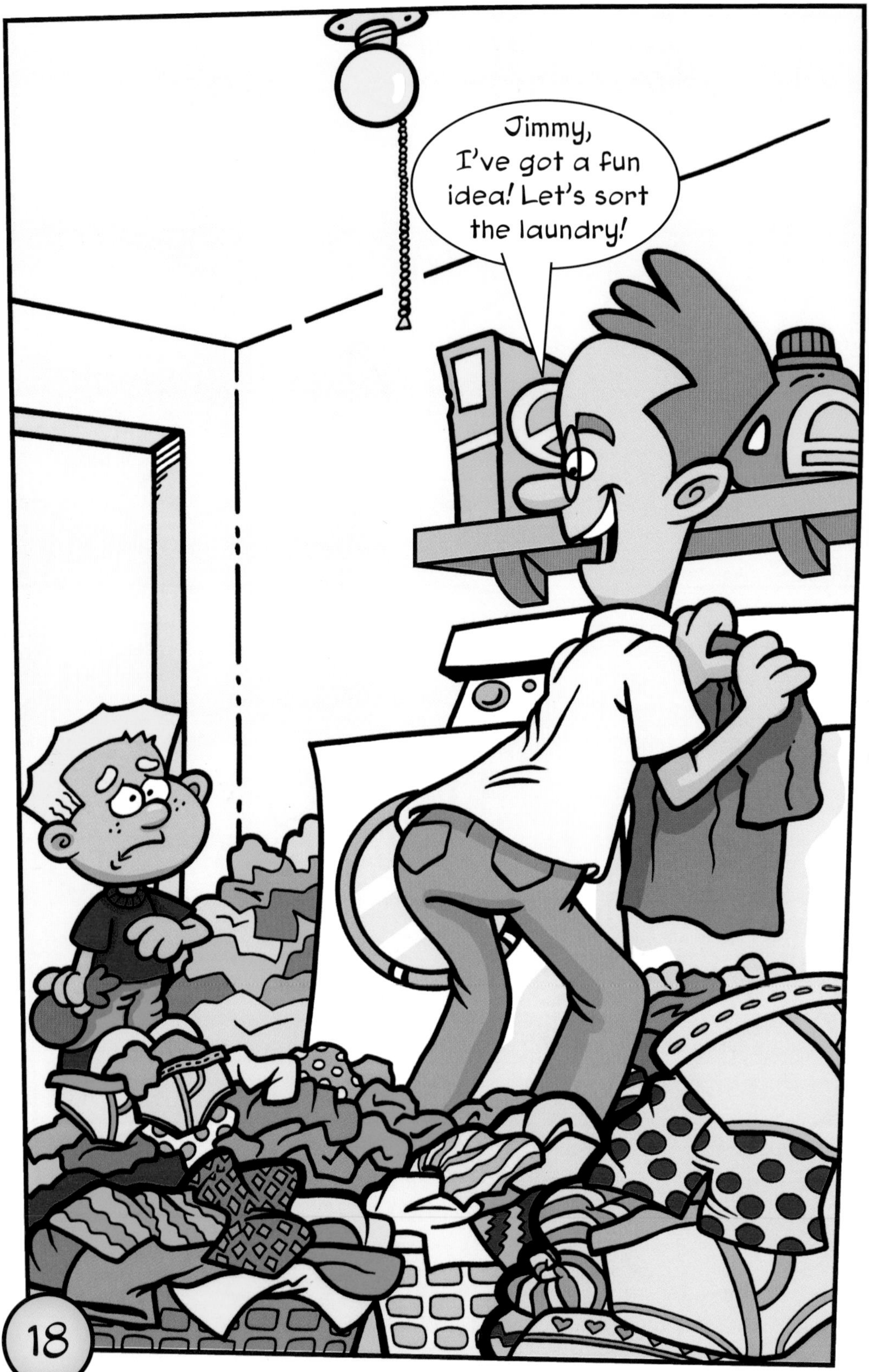
Jimmy, I've got a fun idea! Let's sort the laundry!

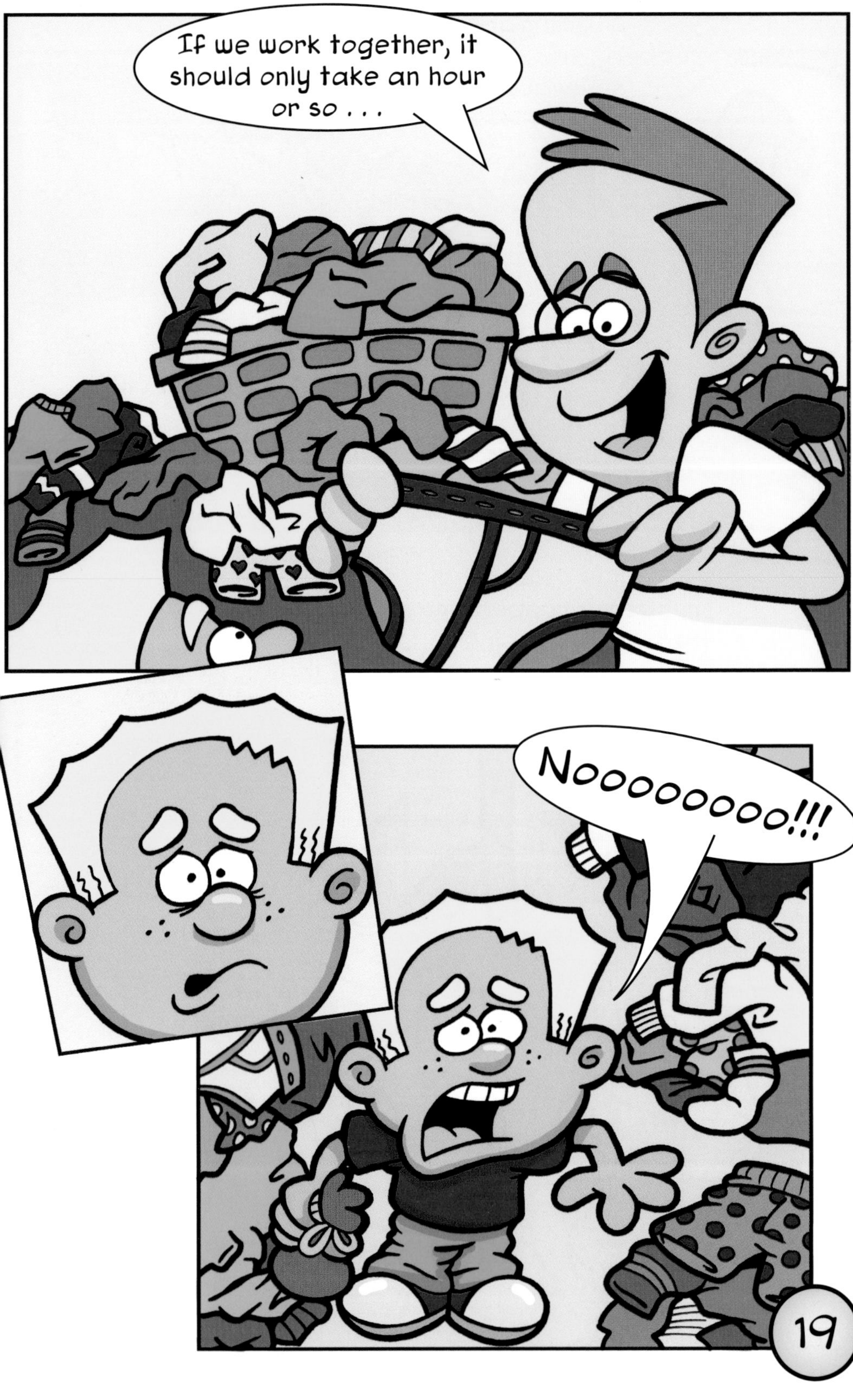
If we work together, it should only take an hour or so . . .
Nooooooooo!!!

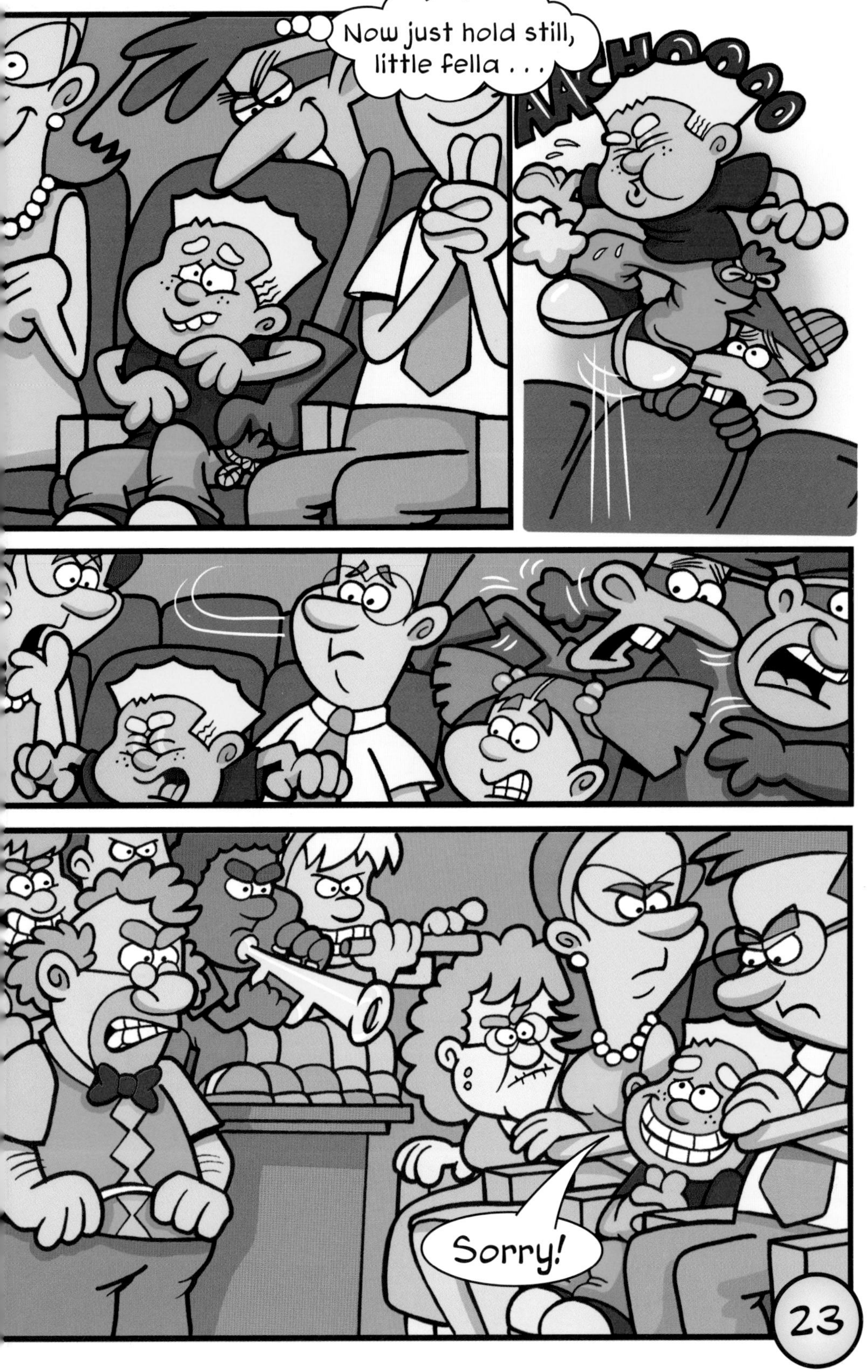

Now just hold still, little fella . . .
AACHOOOOO
Sorry!

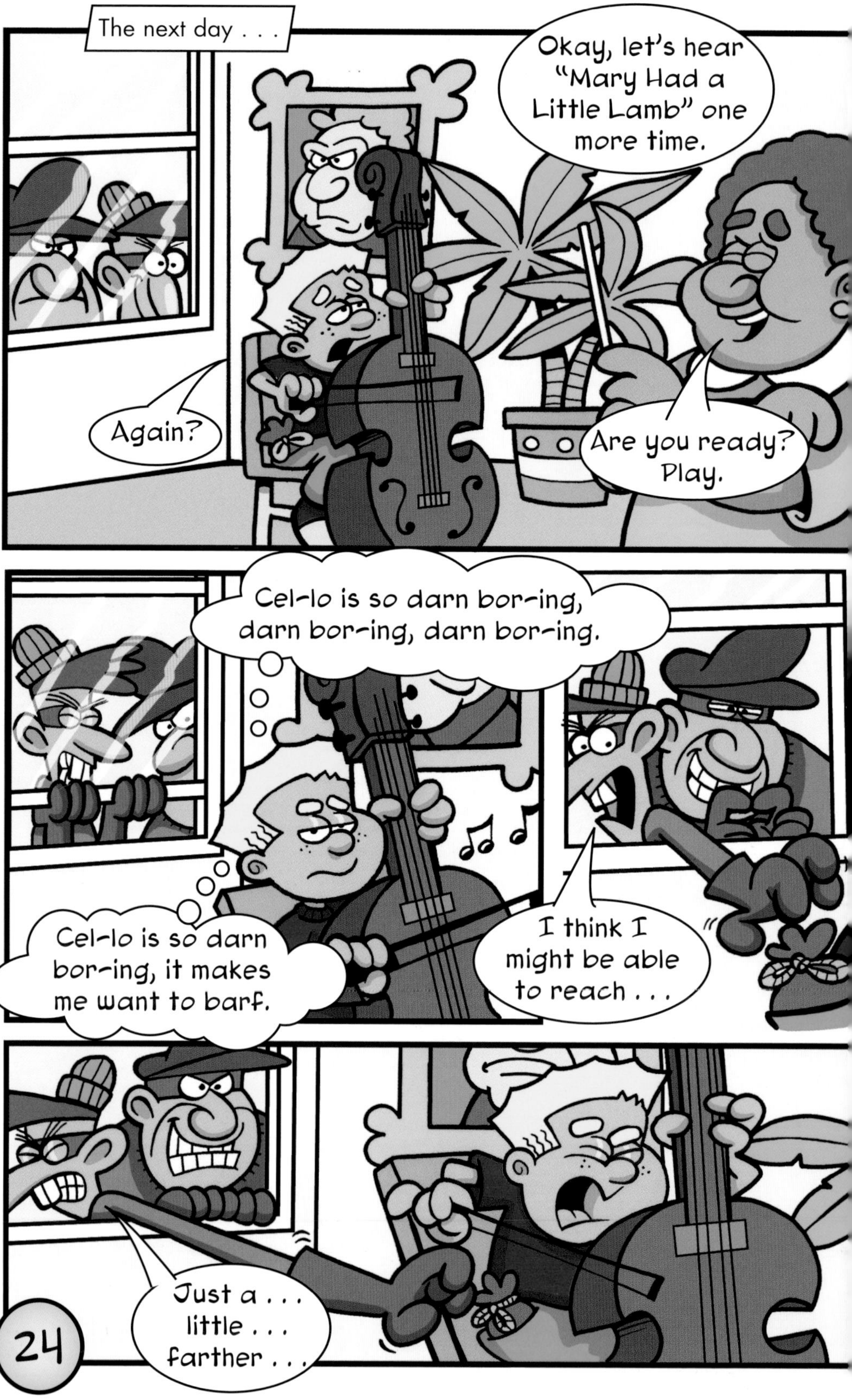
The next day . . .
Okay, let's hear "Mary Had a Little Lamb" one more time.
Again?
Are you ready? Play.
Cel-lo is so darn bor-ing, darn bor-ing, darn bor-ing.
Cel-lo is so darn bor-ing, it makes me want to barf.
I think I might be able to reach . . .
Just a . . . little . . . farther . . .

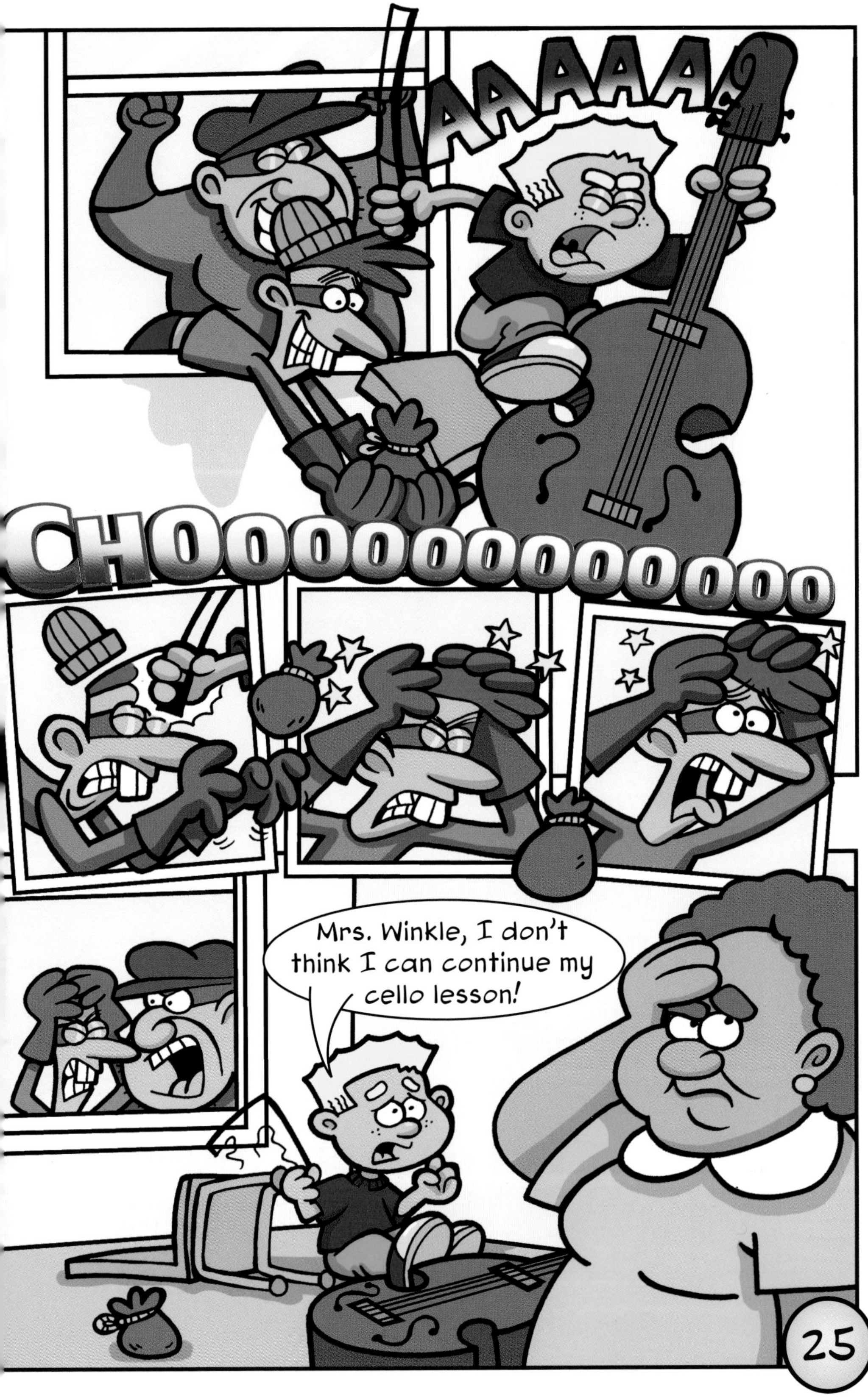
AAAAAA!
CHOOOOOOOOOOOOO
Mrs. Winkle, I don't think I can continue my cello lesson!

26

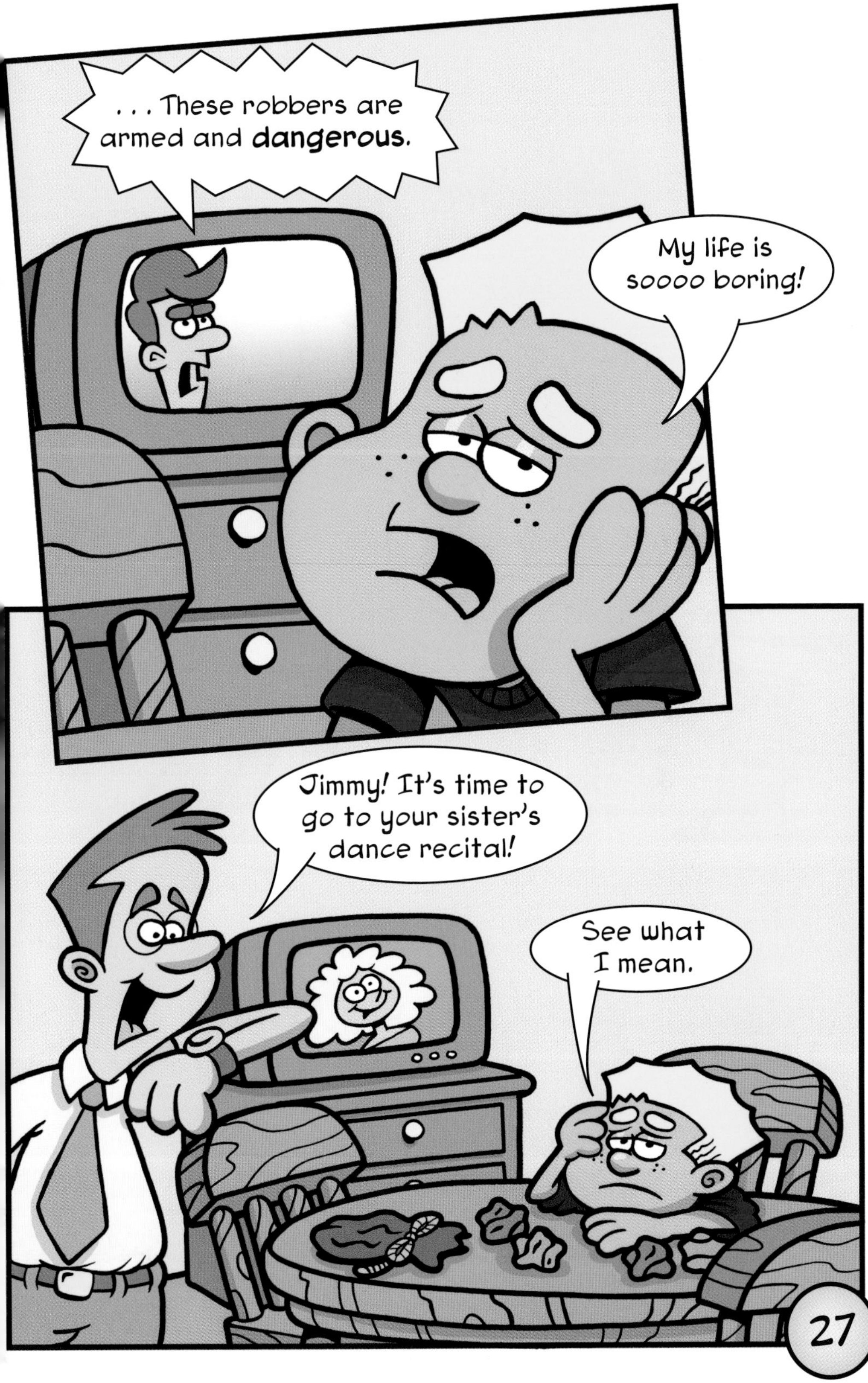
. . . These robbers are armed and **dangerous**.
My life is soooo boring!
Jimmy! It's time to go to your sister's dance recital!
See what I mean.

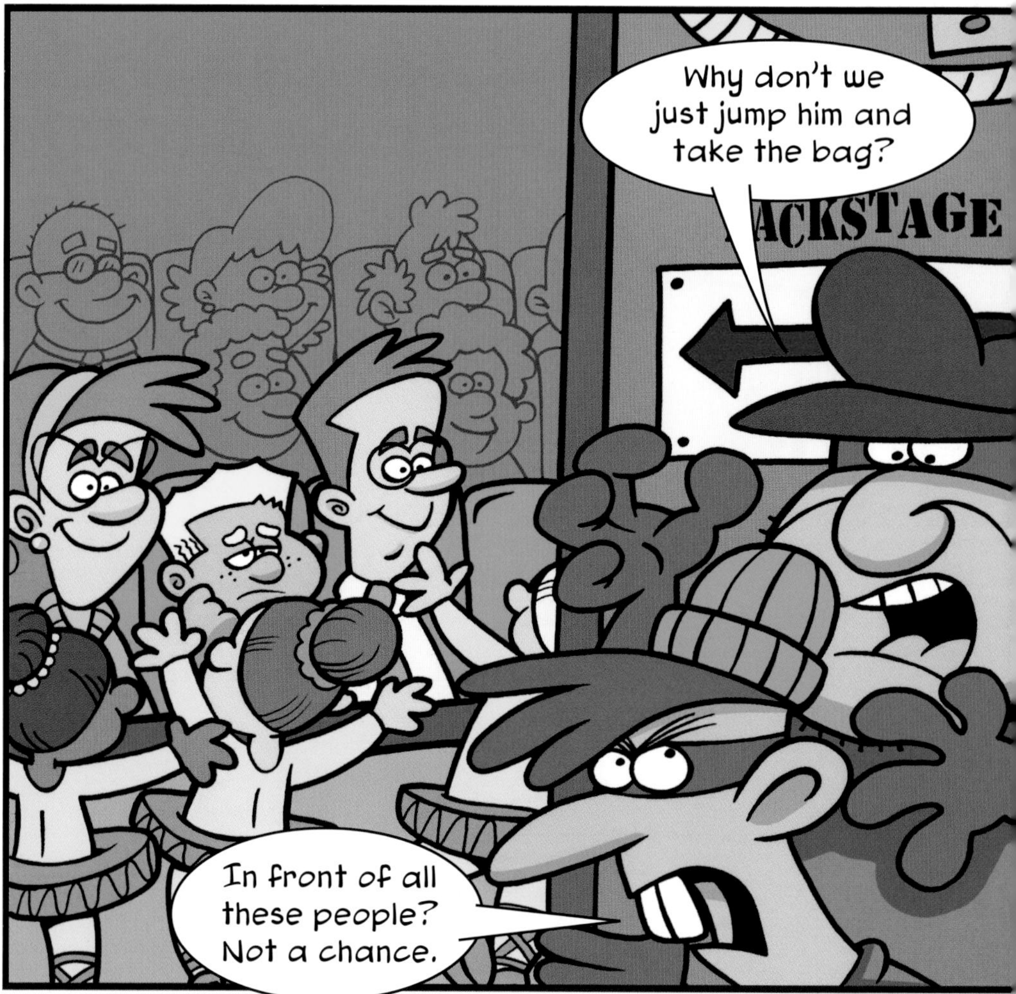
Why don't we just jump him and take the bag?
BACKSTAGE
In front of all these people? Not a chance.

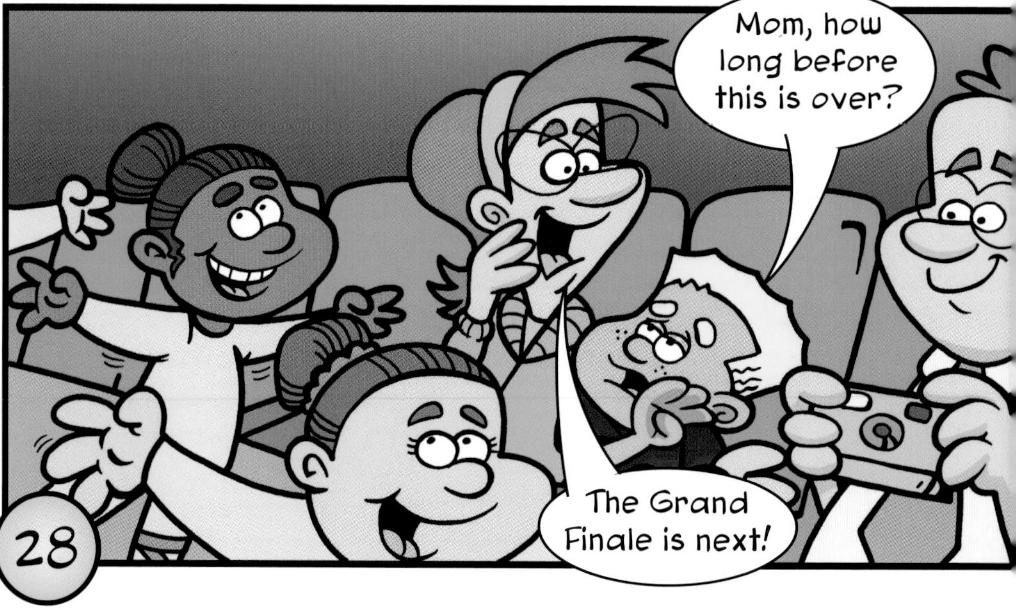
Mom, how long before this is over?
The Grand Finale is next!

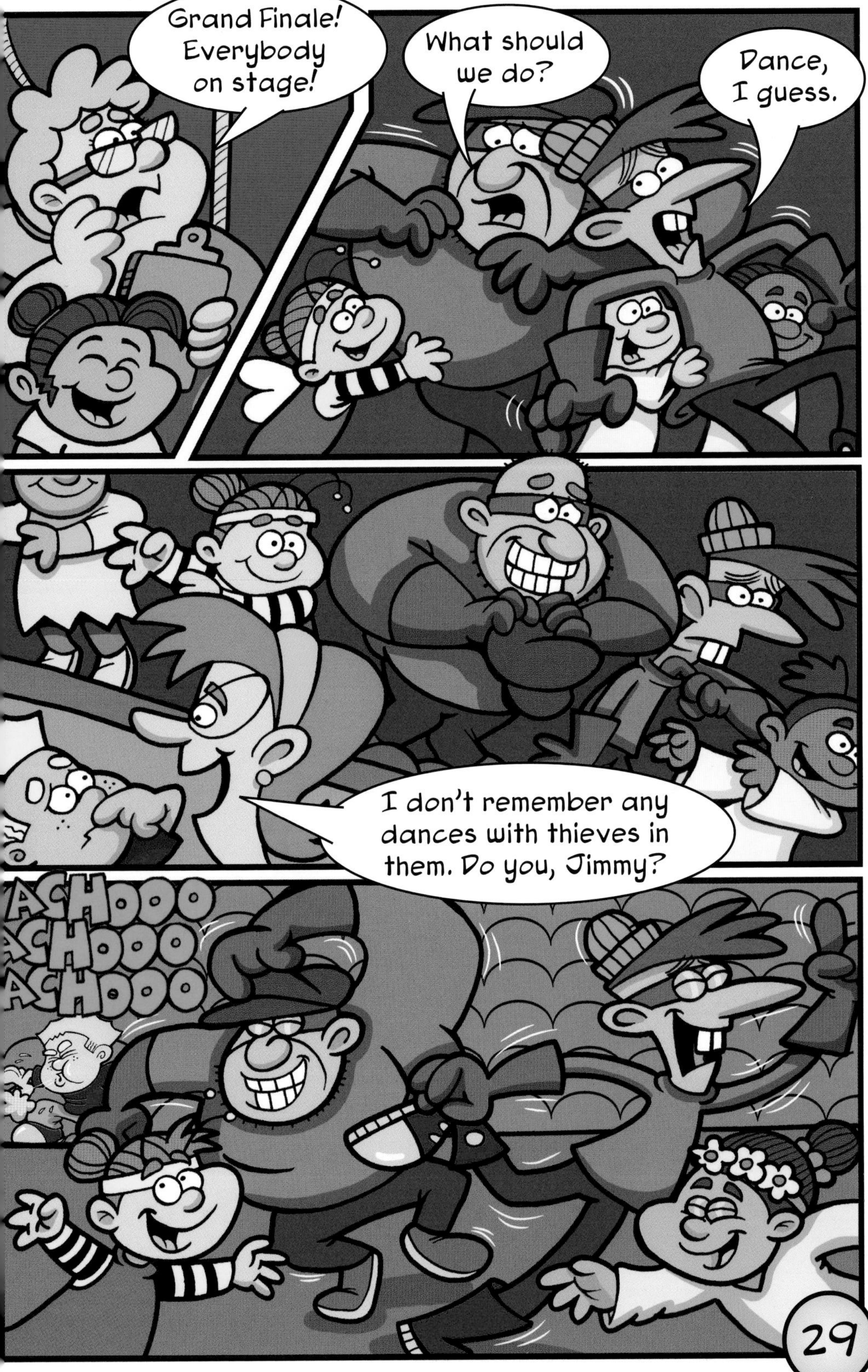
Grand Finale! Everybody on stage!
What should we do?
Dance, I guess.
I don't remember any dances with thieves in them. Do you, Jimmy?
ACHOOO ACHOOO ACHOOO

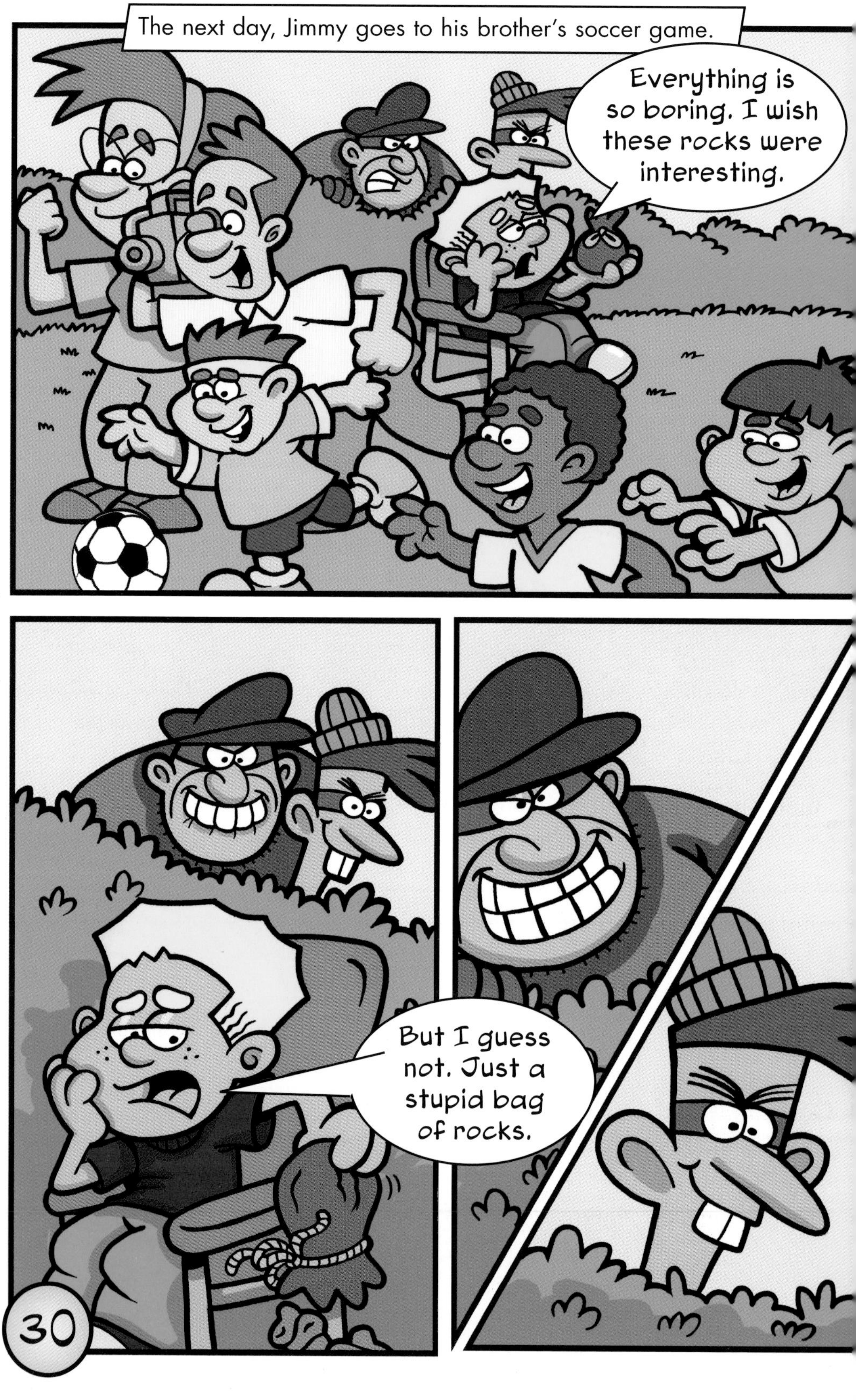
The next day, Jimmy goes to his brother's soccer game.
Everything is so boring. I wish these rocks were interesting.
But I guess not. Just a stupid bag of rocks.

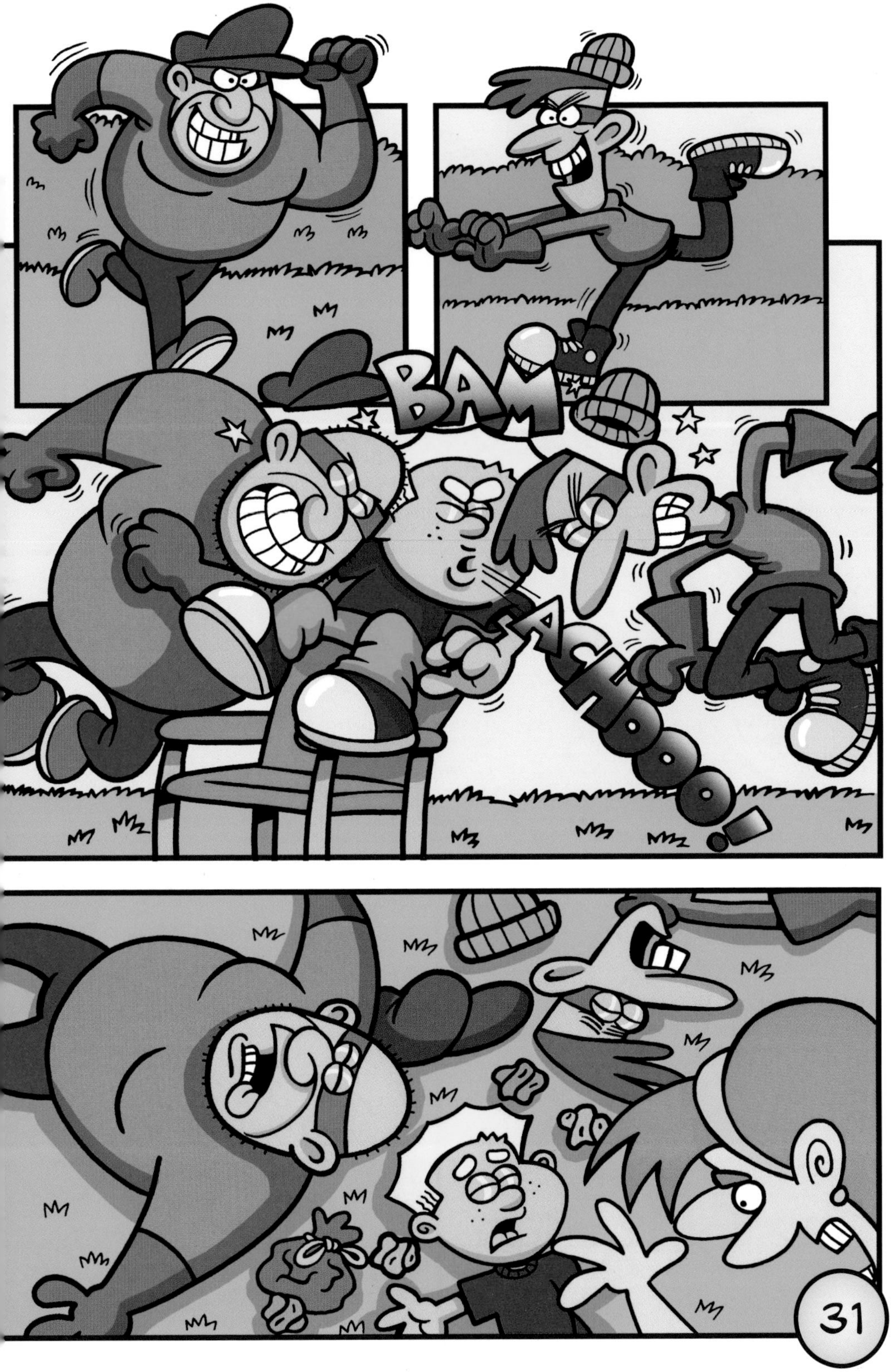
BAM
ACHOOOO!

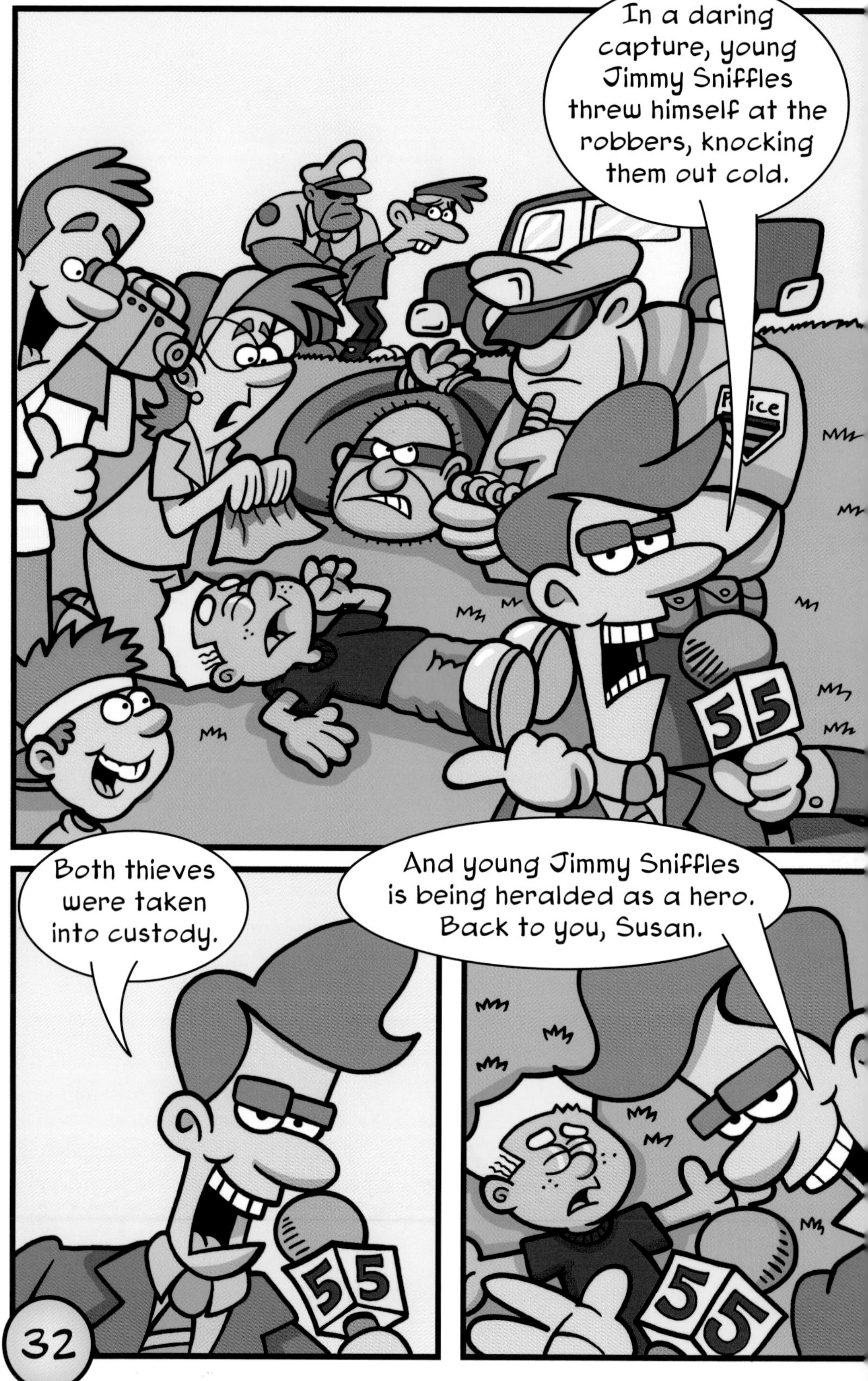
In a daring capture, young Jimmy Sniffles threw himself at the robbers, knocking them out cold.
Both thieves were taken into custody.
And young Jimmy Sniffles is being heralded as a hero. Back to you, Susan.

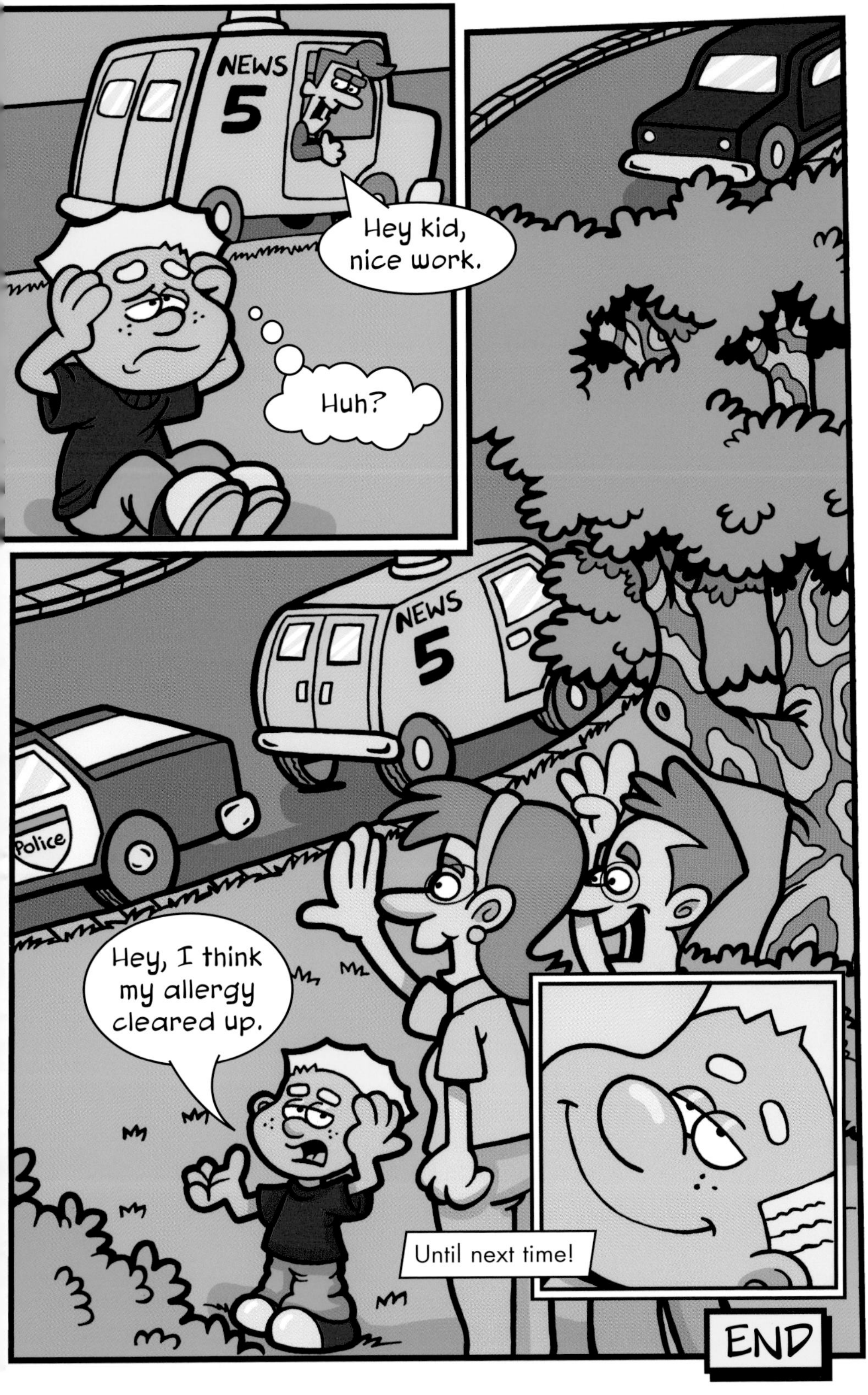
NEWS 5
Hey kid, nice work.
Huh?
NEWS 5
Police
Hey, I think my allergy cleared up.
Until next time!
END

ABOUT THE AUTHOR

Bob Temple has never found a bag of stolen gems, and he's never solved a crime by sneezing, but he has written more than 30 books for children.

ABOUT THE ILLUSTRATOR

Steve Harpster has loved to draw funny cartoons, mean monsters, and goofy gadgets since he was able to pick up a pencil. In first grade, he was able to avoid his writing assignments by working on the pictures for the stories instead.

Steve landed a job drawing funny pictures for books, and that's really what he's best at. Steve lives in Columbus, Ohio, with his wonderful wife, Karen, and their sheepdog, Doodle.

GLOSSARY

agate (AG-it) a stone with bands of color inside

allergy (AL-ur-jee) a bad reaction, such as sneezing, to things like dust, pollen, food, or homework

boring (BOR-ing) doing laundry, watching your brother's band concert or your sister's dance recital, and just about anything else that you **have** to do

errand (AIR-uhnd) going to a place to do something, such as buying a pair of shoes; adults always have errands to do, especially on weekends when they could take you to the zoo or a water park.

gem (JEM) a valuable stone, such as a diamond or ruby

underpants (UHN-dur-pantss) the adult word for underwear; it's easy to remember, kids wear underwear, and adults wear underpants.

Oooh! They look so nice and shiny! Maybe I could polish up my vocabulary with some of these words!

DISCUSSION QUESTIONS

1.) Jimmy doesn't see all the exciting things that happen around him. Why?

2.) Jimmy didn't listen to the news on TV. If he had, he would have realized that the boring rocks he found were really diamonds. If Jimmy had found out, what do you think he would have done with the jewels?

3.) At the beginning of the story, Jimmy doesn't like being allergic to things. Do you think, after he learns about the robbers and jewels, that he will be glad he's allergic?

WRITING PROMPTS

1.) Jimmy hates shopping with his mom. Write about an activity that your mom and dad make you do that is boring. Is there something you could do to make it exciting?

2.) At the end of the story, Jimmy is a hero, except he doesn't know why. Pretend you are Jimmy's friend who has seen everything. Write down what he missed.

3.) While you're out shopping with your family, some careless robbers drop something valuable next to you. Write what you would do next.

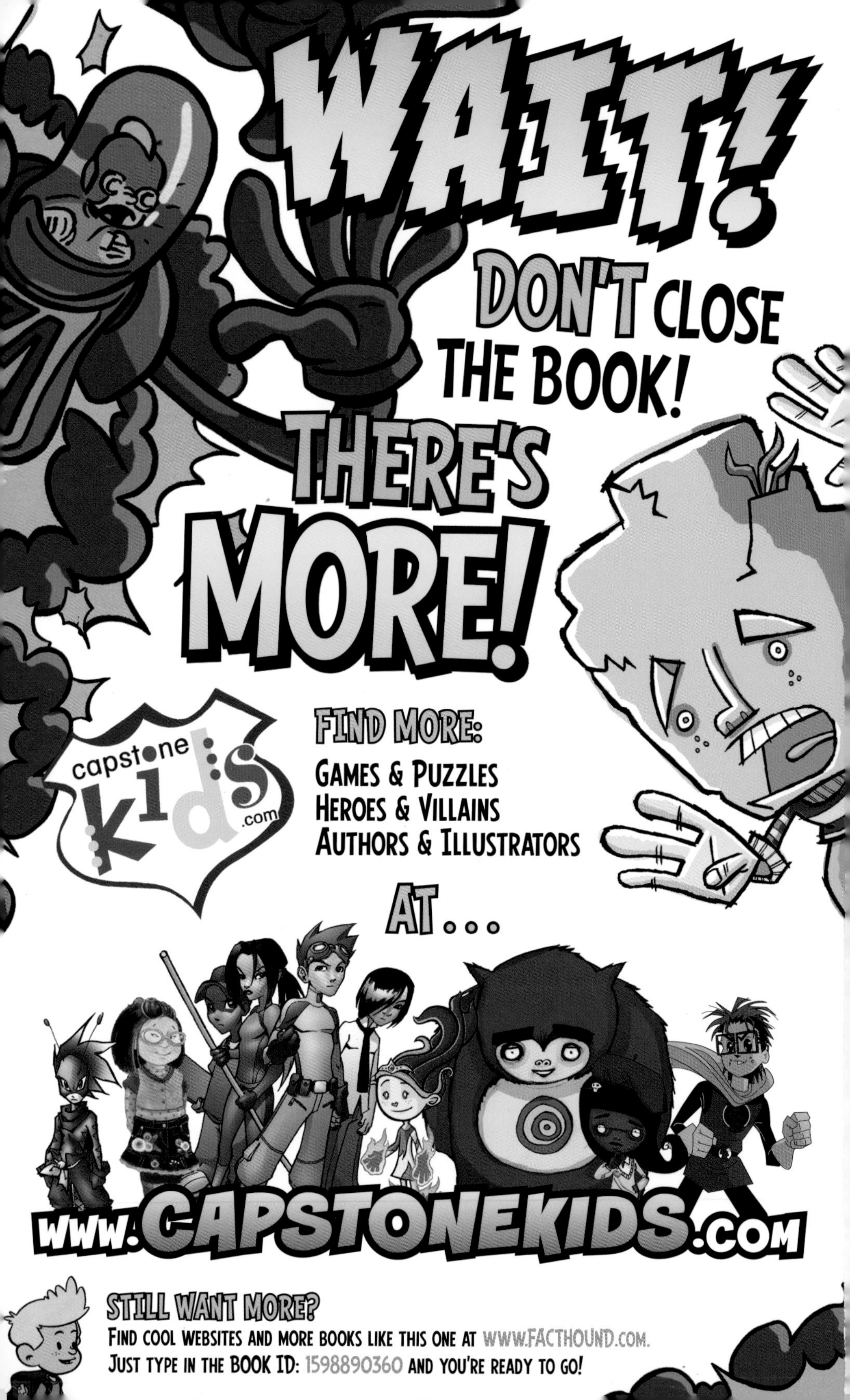
WAIT!
DON'T CLOSE THE BOOK!
THERE'S MORE!
capstone kids .com
FIND MORE:
GAMES & PUZZLES
HEROES & VILLAINS
AUTHORS & ILLUSTRATORS
AT...
WWW.CAPSTONEKIDS.COM
STILL WANT MORE?
FIND COOL WEBSITES AND MORE BOOKS LIKE THIS ONE AT WWW.FACTHOUND.COM.
JUST TYPE IN THE BOOK ID: 1598890360 AND YOU'RE READY TO GO!